The 

STEPHEN LEACOCK was born in Swanmore, Hampshire, England, in 1869. His family emigrated to Canada in 1876 and settled on a farm north of Toronto. Educated at Upper Canada College and the University of Toronto, Leacock pursued graduate studies in economics at the University of Chicago, where he studied under Thorstein Veblen.

Even before he completed his doctorate, Leacock accepted a position as sessional lecturer in political science and economics at McGill University. When he received his Ph.D. in 1903, he was appointed to the full position of lecturer. From 1908 until his retirement in 1936, he chaired the Department of Political Science and Economics.

Leacock's most profitable book was his textbook, *Elements of Political Science*, which was translated into seventeen languages. The author of nineteen books and countless articles on economics, history, and political science, Leacock turned to the writing of humour as his beloved avocation. His first collection of comic stories, *Literary Lapses*, appeared in 1910, and from that time until his death he published a volume of humour almost every year.

Leacock also wrote popular biographies of his two favourite writers, Mark Twain and Charles Dickens. At the time of his death, he left four completed chapters of what was to have been his autobiography. These were published posthumously under the title *The Boy I Left Behind Me*.

Stephen Leacock died in Toronto, Ontario, in 1944.

THE NEW CANADIAN LIBRARY

STEPHEN LEACOCK

Literary Lapses

With an Afterword by Robertson Davies

Canadian Cataloguing in Publication Data

Leacock, Stephen, 1869–1944
Literary lapses

(New Canadian Library)
Bibliography: p.
ISBN 0-7710-9983-5

I. Title. II. Series.

PS8523.E15L58 1989 C818'.5209 C88-094966-X
PR9199.2.L42L58 1989

Printed and bound in Canada

McClelland & Stewart Inc.
The Canadian Publishers
481 University Avenue
Toronto, Ontario
M5G 2E9

Contents

My Financial Career 7
Lord Oxhead's Secret 10
Boarding-House Geometry 17
The Awful Fate of Melpomenus Jones 18
A Christmas Letter 22
How to Make a Million Dollars 23
How to Live to Be 200 28
How to Avoid Getting Married 32
How to Be a Doctor 36
The New Food 40
A New Pathology 42
The Poet Answered 46
The Force of Statistics 48
Men Who Have Shaved Me 49
Getting the Thread of It 54
Telling His Faults 58
Winter Pastimes 60
Number Fifty-Six 64
Aristocratic Education 71
The Conjurer's Revenge 73
Hints to Travellers 76
A Manual of Education 79
Hoodoo McFiggin's Christmas 82
The Life of John Smith 85
On Collecting Things 90
Society Chit-Chat 93

Insurance Up to Date 96
Borrowing a Match 98
A Lesson in Fiction 100
Helping the Armenians 104
A Study in Still Life – The Country Hotel 105
An Experiment with Policeman Hogan 107
The Passing of the Poet 114
Self-made Men 120
A Model Dialogue 123
Back to the Bush 125
Reflections on Riding 131
Saloonio 134
Half-Hours with the Poets –
I. Mr. Wordsworth and the Little Cottage Girl 138
II. How Tennyson Killed the May Queen 141
III. Old Mr. Longfellow on Board the *Hesperus* 144
A, B, and C 147
Afterword 153

MY FINANCIAL CAREER

When I go into a bank I get rattled. The clerks rattle me; the wickets rattle me; the sight of the money rattles me; everything rattles me.

The moment I cross the threshold of a bank and attempt to transact business there, I become an irresponsible idiot.

I knew this beforehand, but my salary had been raised to fifty dollars a month and I felt that the bank was the only place for it.

So I shambled in and looked timidly round at the clerks. I had an idea that a person about to open an account must needs consult the manager.

I went up to a wicket marked "Accountant." The accountant was a tall, cool devil. The very sight of him rattled me. My voice was sepulchral.

"Can I see the manager?" I said, and added solemnly, "alone." I don't know why I said "alone."

"Certainly," said the accountant, and fetched him.

The manager was a grave, calm man. I held my fifty-six dollars clutched in a crumpled ball in my pocket.

"Are you the manager?" I said. God knows I didn't doubt it.

"Yes," he said.

"Can I see you," I asked, "alone?" I didn't want to say "alone" again, but without it the thing seemed self-evident.

The manager looked at me in some alarm. He felt that I had an awful secret to reveal.

"Come in here," he said, and led the way to a private room. He turned the key in the lock.

"We are safe from interruption here," he said. "Sit down."

We both sat down and looked at each other. I found no voice to speak.

"You are one of Pinkerton's men, I presume," he said.

He had gathered from my mysterious manner that I was a detective. I knew what he was thinking, and it made me worse.

"No, not from Pinkerton's," I said, seeming to imply that I came from a rival agency.

"To tell the truth," I went on, as if I had been prompted to lie about it, "I am not a detective at all. I have come to open an account. I intend to keep all my money in this bank."

The manager looked relieved but still serious; he concluded now that I was a son of Baron Rothschild or a young Gould.

"A large account, I suppose," he said.

"Fairly large," I whispered. "I propose to deposit fifty-six dollars now and fifty dollars a month regularly."

The manager got up and opened the door. He called to the accountant.

"Mr. Montgomery," he said unkindly loud, "this gentleman is opening an account, he will deposit fifty-six dollars. Good morning."

I rose.

A big iron door stood open at the side of the room.

"Good morning," I said, and stepped into the safe.

"Come out," said the manager coldly, and showed me the other way.

I went up to the accountant's wicket and poked the

ball of money at him with a quick convulsive movement as if I were doing a conjuring trick.

My face was ghastly pale.

"Here," I said, "deposit it." The tone of the words seemed to mean, "Let us do this painful thing while the fit is on us."

He took the money and gave it to another clerk.

He made me write the sum on a slip and sign my name in a book. I no longer knew what I was doing. The bank swam before my eyes.

"Is it deposited?" I asked in a hollow, vibrating voice.

"It is," said the accountant.

"Then I want to draw a cheque."

My idea was to draw out six dollars of it for present use. Someone gave me a cheque-book through a wicket and someone else began telling me how to write it out. The people in the bank had the impression that I was an invalid millionaire. I wrote something on the cheque and thrust it in at the clerk. He looked at it.

"What! are you drawing it all out again?" he asked in surprise. Then I realised that I had written fifty-six instead of six. I was too far gone to reason now. I had a feeling that it was impossible to explain the thing. All the clerks had stopped writing to look at me.

Reckless with misery, I made a plunge.

"Yes, the whole thing."

"You withdraw your money from the bank?"

"Every cent of it."

"Are you not going to deposit any more?" said the clerk, astonished.

"Never."

An idiot hope struck me that they might think something had insulted me while I was writing the cheque and that I had changed my mind. I made a wretched attempt to look like a man with a fearfully quick temper.

The clerk prepared to pay the money.

"How will you have it?" he said.

"What?"

"How will you have it?"

"Oh"—I caught his meaning and answered without even trying to think—"in fifties."

He gave me a fifty-dollar bill.

"And the six?" he asked dryly.

"In sixes," I said.

He gave it me and I rushed out.

As the big door swung behind me I caught the echo of a roar of laughter that went up to the ceiling of the bank. Since then I bank no more. I keep my money in cash in my trousers pocket and my savings in silver dollars in a sock.

LORD OXHEAD'S SECRET

A ROMANCE IN ONE CHAPTER

It was finished. Ruin had come. Lord Oxhead sat gazing fixedly at the library fire. Without, the wind soughed (or sogged) around the turrets of Oxhead Towers, the seat of the Oxhead family. But the old earl heeded not the sogging of the wind around his seat. He was too absorbed.

Before him lay a pile of blue papers with printed headings. From time to time he turned them over in his hands and replaced them on the table with a groan. To the earl they meant ruin—absolute, irretrievable ruin, and with it the loss of his stately home that had been the pride of the Oxheads for generations. More than that—the world would now know the awful secret of his life.

The earl bowed his head in the bitterness of his sorrow, for he came of a proud stock. About him hung the portraits of his ancestors. Here on the right an Oxhead who had broken his lance at Crécy, or immediately before it. There McWhinnie Oxhead who had ridden madly from the stricken field of Flodden to bring to the affrighted burghers of Edinburgh all the tidings that he had been able to gather in passing the battlefield. Next him hung the dark half Spanish face of Sir Amyas Oxhead of Elizabethan days whose pinnace was the first to dash to Plymouth with the news that the English fleet, as nearly as could be judged from a reasonable distance, seemed about to grapple with the Spanish Armada. Below this, the two Cavalier brothers, Giles and Everard Oxhead, who had sat in the oak with Charles II. Then to the right again the portrait of Sir Ponsonby Oxhead who had fought with Wellington in Spain, and been dismissed for it.

Immediately before the earl as he sat was the family escutcheon emblazoned above the mantelpiece. A child might read the simplicity of its proud significance—an ox rampant quartered in a field of gules with a pike dexter and a dog intermittent in a plain parallelogram right centre, with the motto, "Hic, haec, hoc, hujus, hujus, hujus."

* * * * *

"Father!"—The girl's voice rang clear through the half light of the wainscoted library. Gwendoline Oxhead had thrown herself about the earl's neck. The girl was radiant with happiness. Gwendoline was a beautiful girl of thirty-three, typically English in the freshness of her girlish innocence. She wore one of those charming walking suits of brown holland so fashionable among the aristocracy of England, while a rough leather belt encircled her waist in a single sweep. She bore herself with that sweet simplicity which was her greatest charm. She was probably more simple than any girl of her age for miles around. Gwendoline was the pride of her father's heart, for he saw reflected in her the qualities of his race.

"Father," she said, a blush mantling her fair face, "I am so happy, oh, so happy; Edwin has asked me to be his wife, and we have plighted our troth—at least if you consent. For I will never marry without my father's warrant," she added, raising her head proudly; "I am too much of an Oxhead for that."

Then as she gazed into the old earl's stricken face, the girl's mood changed at once. "Father," she cried, "father, are you ill? What is it? Shall I ring?" As she spoke Gwendoline reached for the heavy bell-rope that hung beside the wall, but the earl, fearful that her frenzied efforts might actually make it ring, checked her hand. "I am, indeed, deeply troubled," said Lord Oxhead, "but of that anon. Tell me first what is this news you bring. I hope, Gwendoline, that your choice has been worthy of an Oxhead, and that he to whom you have plighted your troth will be worthy to bear our motto with his own." And, raising his eyes to the escutcheon before him, the earl murmured half unconsciously, "Hic, haec, hoc, hujus, hujus, hujus," breathing perhaps a prayer as many of his ancestors had done before him that he might never forget it.

"Father," continued Gwendoline, half timidly, "Edwin is an American."

"You surprise me indeed," answered Lord Oxhead; "and yet," he continued, turning to his daughter with the courtly grace that marked the nobleman of the old school, "why should we not respect and admire the Americans? Surely there have been great names among them. Indeed, our ancestor Sir Amyas Oxhead was, I think, married to Pocahontas—at least if not actually married"—the earl hesitated a moment.

"At least they loved one another," said Gwendoline simply.

"Precisely," said the earl, with relief, "they loved one another, yes, exactly." Then, as if musing to himself, "Yes, there have been great Americans. Bolivar was an American. The two Washingtons—George and Booker—are both Americans. There have been others, too, though for the moment I do not recall their names. But tell me, Gwendoline, this Edwin of yours—where is his family seat?"

"It is at Oshkosh, Wisconsin, father."

"Ah! Say you so?" rejoined the earl, with rising interest. "Oshkosh is, indeed, a grand old name. The Oshkosh are a Russian family. An Ivan Oshkosh came to England with Peter the Great and married my ancestress. Their descendant in the second degree once removed, Mixtup Oshkosh, fought at the burning of Moscow and later at the sack of Salamanca and the treaty of Adrianople. And Wisconsin, too," the old nobleman went on, his features kindling with animation, for he had a passion for heraldry, genealogy, chronology, and commercial geography; "the Wisconsins, or better, I think, the Guisconsins, are of old blood. A Guisconsin followed Henry I to Jerusalem and rescued my ancestor Hardup Oxhead from the Saracens. Another Guisconsin . . ."

"Nay, father," said Gwendoline, gently interrupting, "Wisconsin is not Edwin's own name: that is, I believe, the name of his estate. My lover's name is Edwin Einstein."

"Einstein," repeated the earl dubiously—"an Indian name perhaps; yet the Indians are many of them of excellent family. An ancestor of mine . . ."

"Father," said Gwendoline, again interrupting, "here is a portrait of Edwin. Judge for yourself if he be noble." With this she placed in her father's hand an American tin-type, tinted in pink and brown. The picture represented a typical specimen of American manhood of that Anglo-Semitic type so often seen in persons of mixed English and Jewish extraction. The figure was well over five feet two inches in height and broad in proportion. The graceful sloping shoulders harmonised with the slender and well-poised waist, and with a hand pliant and yet prehensile. The pallor of the features was relieved by a drooping black moustache.

Such was Edwin Einstein, to whom Gwendoline's heart, if not her hand, was already affianced. Their love had been so simple and yet so strange. It seemed to Gwendoline that it was but a thing of yesterday, and yet in reality they had met three weeks ago. Love had drawn them irresistibly together. To Edwin, the fair English girl with her old name and wide estates possessed a charm that he scarcely dared to confess to himself. He determined to woo her. To Gwendoline there was that in Edwin's bearing, the rich jewels that he wore, the vast fortune that rumour ascribed to him, that appealed to something romantic and chivalrous in her nature. She loved to hear him speak of stocks and bonds, corners and margins, and his father's colossal business. It all seemed so noble and so far above the sordid lives of the people about her. Edwin, too, loved to hear the girl talk of her father's estates, of the diamond-hilted sword that the Saladin had given, or had lent, to her ancestor hundreds of years ago. Her description of her father, the old earl, touched something romantic in Edwin's generous heart. He was never tired of asking how old he was, was he robust, did a shock, a sudden shock, affect him much? And so on. Then had come the evening that Gwendoline loved to live over and over again in her mind, when Edwin had asked her in his straightforward, manly way, whether—subject to certain written stipulations to be considered later—she would be his wife: and she, putting her hand confidingly in his hand, answered simply, that—subject to the consent of her father and pending always the necessary legal formalities and inquiries—she would.

It had all seemed like a dream: and now Edwin Einstein had come in person to ask her hand from the earl, her father. Indeed, he was at this moment in the outer hall testing the gold leaf in the picture-frames with his pen-knife while waiting for his affianced to break the fateful news to Lord Oxhead.

Gwendoline summoned her courage for a great effort. "Papa," she said, "there is one other thing that it is fair to tell you. Edwin's father is in business."

The earl started from his seat in blank amazement. "In business!" he repeated. "The father of the suitor of the daughter of an Oxhead in business! My daughter the stepdaughter of the grandfather of my grandson! Are you mad, girl? It is too much, too much!"

"But, father," pleaded the beautiful girl in anguish, "hear me. It is Edwin's father—Sarcophagus Einstein, senior—not Edwin himself. Edwin does nothing. He has never earned a penny. He is quite unable to support himself. You have only to see him to believe it. Indeed, dear father, he is just like us. He is here now, in this house, waiting to see you. If it were not for his great wealth . . ."

"Girl," said the earl sternly, "I care not for the man's riches. How much has he?"

"Fifteen million, two hundred and fifty thousand dollars," answered Gwendoline. Lord Oxhead leaned his head against the mantelpiece. His mind was in a whirl. He was trying to calculate the yearly interest on fifteen and a quarter million dollars at four and a half per cent reduced to pounds, shillings, and pence. It was bootless. His brain, trained by long years of high living and plain thinking, had become too subtle, too refined an instrument for arithmetic. . . .

At this moment the door opened and Edwin Einstein stood before the earl. Gwendoline never forgot what happened. Through her life the picture of it haunted her —her lover upright at the door, his fine frank gaze fixed inquiringly on the diamond pin in her father's necktie, and he, her father, raising from the mantelpiece a face of agonised amazement.

"You! You!" he gasped. For a moment he stood to his full height, swaying and groping in the air, then fell prostrate his full length upon the floor. The lovers rushed to his aid. Edwin tore open his neckcloth and plucked aside his diamond pin to give him air. But it was too late. Earl Oxhead had breathed his last. Life had fled. The earl was extinct. That is to say, he was dead.

The reason of his death was never known. Had the sight of Edwin killed him? It might have. The old family doctor, hurriedly summoned, declared his utter ignorance. This, too, was likely. Edwin himself could explain nothing. But it was observed that after the earl's death and his marriage with Gwendoline he was a changed man; he dressed better, talked much better English.

The wedding itself was quiet, almost sad. At Gwendoline's request there was no wedding breakfast, no bridesmaids, and no reception, while Edwin, respecting his bride's bereavement, insisted that there should be no best man, no flowers, no presents, and no honeymoon.

Thus Lord Oxhead's secret died with him. It was probably too complicated to be interesting anyway.

BOARDING-HOUSE GEOMETRY

DEFINITIONS AND AXIOMS

ALL boarding-houses are the same boarding-house.

Boarders in the same boarding-house and on the same flat are equal to one another.

A single room is that which has no parts and no magnitude.

The landlady of a boarding-house is a parallelogram —that is, an oblong angular figure, which cannot be described, but which is equal to anything.

A wrangle is the disinclination of two boarders to each other that meet together but are not in the same line.

All the other rooms being taken, a single room is said to be a double room.

POSTULATES AND PROPOSITIONS

A pie may be produced any number of times.

The landlady can be reduced to her lowest terms by a series of propositions.

A bee-line may be made from any boarding-house to any other boarding-house.

The clothes of a boarding-house bed, though produced ever so far both ways, will not meet.

Any two meals at a boarding-house are together less than two square meals.

If from the opposite ends of a boarding-house a line be drawn passing through all the rooms in turn, then the stovepipe which warms the boarders will lie within that line.

On the same bill and on the same side of it there should not be two charges for the same thing.

If there be two boarders on the same flat, and the amount of side of the one be equal to the amount of side of the other, each to each, and the wrangle between one boarder and the landlady be equal to the wrangle between the landlady and the other, then shall the weekly bills of the two boarders be equal also, each to each.

For if not, let one bill be the greater.

Then the other bill is less than it might have been—which is absurd.

THE AWFUL FATE OF MELPOMENUS JONES

SOME people—not you nor I, because we are so awfully self-possessed—but some people, find great difficulty in saying good-bye when making a call or spending the evening. As the moment draws near when the visitor feels that he is fairly entitled to go away he rises and says abruptly, "Well, I think I . . ." Then the people say, "Oh, must you go now? Surely it's early yet!" And a pitiful struggle ensues.

I think the saddest case of this kind of thing that I ever knew was that of my poor friend Melpomenus Jones, a curate—such a dear young man, and only twenty-three! He simply couldn't get away from people. He was too modest to tell a lie, and too religious to wish to appear rude. Now it happened that he went to call on some friends of his on the very first afternoon of his summer vacation. The next six weeks were entirely his own—absolutely nothing to do. He chatted awhile, drank two cups of tea, then braced himself for the effort and said suddenly:

"Well, I think I . . ."

But the lady of the house said, "Oh, no! Mr. Jones, can't you really stay a little longer?"

Jones was always truthful. "Oh, yes," he said, "of course, I—er—can stay."

"Then please don't go."

He stayed. He drank eleven cups of tea. Night was falling. He rose again.

"Well, now," he said shyly, "I think I really . . ."

"You must go?" said the lady politely. "I thought perhaps you could have stayed to dinner. . . ."

"Oh, well, so I could, you know," Jones said, "if . . ."

"Then please stay, I'm sure my husband will be delighted."

"All right," he said feebly, "I'll stay," and he sank back into his chair, just full of tea, and miserable.

Papa came home. They had dinner. All through the meal Jones sat planning to leave at eight-thirty. All the family wondered whether Mr. Jones was stupid and sulky, or only stupid.

After dinner mamma undertook to "draw him out," and showed him photographs. She showed him all the family museum, several gross of them—photos of papa's uncle and his wife, and mamma's brother and his little boy, an awfully interesting photo of papa's uncle's friend in his Bengal uniform, an awfully well-taken photo of papa's grandfather's partner's dog, and an awfully wicked one of papa as the devil for a fancy-dress ball.

At eight-thirty Jones had examined seventy-one photographs. There were about sixty-nine more that he hadn't. Jones rose.

"I must say good night now," he pleaded.

"Say good night!" they said, "why, it's only half-past eight! Have you anything to do?"

"Nothing," he admitted, and muttered something about staying six weeks, and then laughed miserably.

Just then it turned out that the favourite child of the family, such a dear little romp, had hidden Mr. Jones's hat; so papa said that he must stay, and invited him to a pipe and a chat. Papa had the pipe and gave Jones the chat, and still he stayed. Every moment he meant to take the plunge, but couldn't. Then papa began to get very tired of Jones, and fidgeted and finally said with jocular irony, that Jones had better stay all night, they could give him a shake-down. Jones mistook his meaning and thanked him with tears in his eyes, and papa put Jones to bed in the spare room and cursed him heartily.

After breakfast next day, papa went off to his work in the City, and left Jones playing with the baby, broken-hearted. His nerve was utterly gone. He was meaning to leave all day, but the thing had got on his mind and he simply couldn't. When papa came home in the evening he was surprised and chagrined to find Jones still there. He thought to jockey him out with a jest, and said he thought he'd have to charge him for his board, he! he! The unhappy young man stared wildly for a moment, then wrung papa's hand, paid him a month's board in advance, and broke down and sobbed like a child.

In the days that followed he was moody and unapproachable. He lived, of course, entirely in the drawing-room, and the lack of air and exercise began to tell sadly on his health. He passed his time in drinking tea and looking at the photographs. He would stand for hours gazing at the photographs of papa's uncle's friend in his Bengal uniform—talking to it, sometimes swearing bitterly at it. His mind was visibly failing.

At length the crash came. They carried him upstairs in a raging delirium of fever. The illness that followed was terrible. He recognised no one, not even papa's uncle's friend in his Bengal uniform. At times he would start up from his bed and shriek, "Well, I think I . . ." and then fall back upon the pillows with a horrible laugh. Then, again, he would leap up and cry, "Another cup of tea and more photographs! More photographs! Har! Har!"

At length, after a month of agony, on the last day of his vacation, he passed away. They say that when the last moment came, he sat up in bed with a beautiful smile of confidence playing upon his face, and said, "Well—the angels are calling me; I'm afraid I really must go now. Good afternoon."

And the rushing of his spirit from its prison-house was as rapid as a hunted cat passing over a garden fence.

A CHRISTMAS LETTER

(In answer to a young lady who has sent an invitation to be present at a children's party)

MADEMOISELLE,

Allow me very gratefully but firmly to refuse your kind invitation. You doubtless mean well; but your ideas are unhappily mistaken.

Let us understand one another once and for all. I cannot at my mature age participate in the sports of children with such abandon as I could wish. I entertain, and have always entertained, the sincerest regard for such games as Hunt-the-Slipper and Blind-Man's Buff. But I have now reached a time of life, when, to have my eyes blindfolded and to have a powerful boy of ten hit me in the back with a hobby-horse and ask me to guess who hit me, provokes me to a fit of retaliation which could only culminate in reckless criminality. Nor can I cover my shoulders with a drawing-room rug and crawl round on my hands and knees under the pretence that I am a bear without a sense of personal insufficiency, which is painful to me.

Neither can I look on with a complacent eye at the sad spectacle of your young clerical friend, the Reverend Mr. Uttermost Farthing, abandoning himself to such gambols and appearing in the rôle of life and soul of the evening. Such a degradation of his holy calling grieves me, and I cannot but suspect him of ulterior motives.

You inform me that your maiden aunt intends to help you entertain the party. I have not, as you know, the honour of your aunt's acquaintance, yet I think I may with reason surmise that she will organise games—guessing games—in which she will ask me to name a river in Asia beginning with a Z; on my failure to do so she will put a hot plate down my neck as a forfeit, and the children will clap their hands. These games, my dear young friend, involve the use of a more adaptable intellect than mine, and I cannot consent to be a party to them.

May I say in conclusion that I do not consider a five-cent pen-wiper from the top branch of a Xmas tree any adequate compensation for the kind of evening you propose.

I have the honour
To subscribe myself,
Your obedient servant.

HOW TO MAKE A MILLION DOLLARS

I MIX a good deal with the millionaires. I like them. I like their faces. I like the way they live. I like the things they eat. The more we mix together the better I like the things we mix.

Especially I like the way they dress, their grey check trousers, their white check waistcoats, their heavy gold chains, and the signet-rings that they sign their cheques with. My! they look nice. Get six or seven of them sitting together in the club and it's a treat to see them. And if they get the least dust on them, men come and brush it off. Yes, and are glad to. I'd like to take some of the dust off them myself.

Even more than what they eat I like their intellectual

grasp. It is wonderful. Just watch them read. They simply read all the time. Go into the club at any hour and you'll see three or four of them at it. And the things they can read! You'd think that a man who's been driving hard in the office from eleven o'clock until three, with only an hour and a half for lunch, would be too fagged. Not a bit. These men can sit down after office hours and read the *Sketch* and the *Police Gazette* and the *Pink Un,* and understand the jokes just as well as I can.

What I love to do is to walk up and down among them and catch the little scraps of conversation. The other day I heard one lean forward and say, "Well, I offered him a million and a half and said I wouldn't give a cent more, he could either take it or leave it——" I just longed to break in and say, "What! what! a million and a half! Oh! say that again! Offer it to me, to either take it or leave it. Do try me once: I know I can: or here, make it a plain million and let's call it done."

Not that these men are careless over money. No, sir. Don't think it. Of course they don't take much account of big money, a hundred thousand dollars at a shot or anything of that sort. But little money. You've no idea till you know them how anxious they get about a cent, or half a cent, or less.

Why, two of them came into the club the other night just frantic with delight: they said wheat had risen and they'd cleaned up four cents each in less than half an hour. They bought a dinner for sixteen on the strength of it. I don't understand it. I've often made twice as much as that writing for the papers and never felt like boasting about it.

One night I heard one man say, "Well, let's call up New York and offer them a quarter of a cent." Great heavens! Imagine paying the cost of calling up New York, nearly five million people, late at night and offering them a quarter of a cent! And yet—did New York get mad? No, they took it. Of course, it's high finance. I don't pretend to understand it. I tried after that to call up Chicago and offer it a cent and a half, and to call up Hamilton, Ontario, and offer it half a dollar, and the operator only thought I was crazy.

All this shows, of course, that I've been studying how the millionaires do it. I have. For years. I thought it might be helpful to young men just beginning to work and anxious to stop.

You know, many a man realises late in life that if when he was a boy he had known what he knows now, instead of being what he is he might be what he won't; but how few boys stop to think that if they knew what they don't know instead of being what they will be, they wouldn't be? These are awful thoughts.

At any rate, I've been gathering hints on how it is they do it.

One thing I'm sure about. If a young man wants to make a million dollars he's got to be mighty careful about his diet and his living. This may seem hard. But success is only achieved with pains.

There is no use in a young man who hopes to make a million dollars thinking he's entitled to get up at 7.30, eat Force and poached eggs, drink cold water at lunch, and go to bed at 10 p.m. You can't do it. I've seen too many millionaires for that. If you want to be a millionaire you mustn't get up till ten in the morning. They never do. They daren't. It would be as much as their business is worth if they were seen on the street at half-past nine.

And the old idea of abstemiousness is all wrong. To

be a millionaire you need champagne, lots of it and all the time. That and Scotch whisky and soda: you have to sit up nearly all night and drink buckets of it. This is what clears the brain for business next day. I've seen some of these men with their brains so clear in the morning, that their faces look positively boiled.

To live like this requires, of course, resolution. But you can buy that by the pint.

Therefore, my dear young man, if you want to get moved on from your present status in business, change your life. When your landlady brings your bacon and eggs for breakfast, throw them out the window to the dog and tell her to bring you some chilled asparagus and a pint of Moselle. Then telephone to your employer that you'll be down about eleven o'clock. You will get moved on. Yes, very quickly.

Just how the millionaires make the money is a difficult question. But one way is this. Strike the town with five cents in your pocket. They nearly all do this; they've told me again and again (men with millions and millions) that the first time they struck town they had only five cents. That seems to have given them their start. Of course, it's not easy to do. I've tried it several times. I nearly did it once. I borrowed five cents, carried it away out of town with an awful rush. If I hadn't struck a beer saloon in the suburbs and spent the five cents I might have been rich to-day.

Another good plan is to start something. Something on a huge scale: something nobody ever thought of. For instance, one man I know told me that once he was down in Mexico without a cent (he'd lost his five in striking Central America) and he noticed that they had no power plants. So he started some and made a mint of money. Another man that I know was once stranded in New

York, absolutely without a nickel. Well, it occurred to him that what was needed were buildings ten stories higher than any that had been put up. So he built two and sold them right away. Ever so many millionaires begin in some such simple way as that.

There is, of course, a much easier way than any of these. I almost hate to tell this, because I want to do it myself.

I learned of it just by chance one night at the club. There is one old man there, extremely rich, with one of the best faces of the lot, just like a hyena. I never used to know how he had got so rich. So one evening I asked one of the millionaires how old Bloggs had made all his money.

"How he made it?" he answered with a sneer. "Why, he made it by taking it out of widows and orphans."

Widows and orphans! I thought, what an excellent idea. But who would have suspected that they had it?

"And how," I asked pretty cautiously, "did he go at it to get it out of them?"

"Why," the man answered, "he just ground them under his heels, that was how."

Now isn't that simple? I've thought of that conversation often since and I mean to try it. If I can get hold of them, I'll grind them quick enough. But how to get them. Most of the widows I know look pretty solid for that sort of thing, and as for orphans, it must take an awful lot of them. Meantime I am waiting, and if I ever get a large bunch of orphans all together, I'll stamp on them and see.

I find, too, on inquiry, that you can also grind it out of clergymen. They say they grind nicely. But perhaps orphans are easier.

HOW TO LIVE TO BE 200

TWENTY years ago I knew a man called Jiggins, who had the Health Habit.

He used to take a cold plunge every morning. He said it opened his pores. After it he took a hot sponge. He said it closed the pores. He got so that he could open and shut his pores at will.

Jiggins used to stand and breathe at an open window for half an hour before dressing. He said it expanded his lungs. He might, of course, have had it done in a shoe-store with a boot-stretcher, but after all it cost him nothing this way, and what is half an hour?

After he had got his undershirt on, Jiggins used to hitch himself up like a dog in harness and do Sandow exercises. He did them forwards, backwards, and hind-side up.

He could have got a job as a dog anywhere. He spent all his time at this kind of thing. In his spare time at the office, he used to lie on his stomach on the floor and see if he could lift himself up with his knuckles. If he could, then he tried some other way until he found one that he couldn't do. Then he would spend the rest of his lunch hour on his stomach, perfectly happy.

In the evenings in his room he used to lift iron bars, cannon-balls, heave dumb-bells, and haul himself up to the ceiling with his teeth. You could hear the thumps half a mile.

He liked it.

He spent half the night slinging himself around his room. He said it made his brain clear. When he got his brain perfectly clear, he went to bed and slept. As soon as he woke, he began clearing it again.

Jiggins is dead. He was, of course, a pioneer, but the fact that he dumb-belled himself to death at an early age does not prevent a whole generation of young men from following in his path.

They are ridden by the Health Mania.

They make themselves a nuisance.

They get up at impossible hours. They go out in silly little suits and run Marathon heats before breakfast. They chase around barefoot to get the dew on their feet. They hunt for ozone. They bother about pepsin. They won't eat meat because it has too much nitrogen. They won't eat fruit because it hasn't any. They prefer albumen and starch and nitrogen to huckleberry pie and doughnuts. They won't drink water out of a tap. They won't eat sardines out of a can. They won't use oysters out of a pail. They won't drink milk out of a glass. They are afraid of alcohol in any shape. Yes, sir, afraid. "Cowards."

And after all their fuss they presently incur some simple old-fashioned illness and die like anybody else.

Now people of this sort have no chance to attain any great age. They are on the wrong track.

Listen. Do you want to live to be really old, to enjoy a grand, green, exuberant, boastful old age and to make yourself a nuisance to your whole neighbourhood with your reminiscences?

Then cut out all this nonsense. Cut it out. Get up in the morning at a sensible hour. The time to get up is when you have to, not before. If your office opens at eleven, get up at ten-thirty. Take your chance on ozone. There isn't any such thing anyway. Or, if there is, you can buy a thermos bottle full for five cents, and put it on a shelf in your cupboard. If your work begins at seven in the morning, get up at ten minutes to, but don't be liar enough to say that you like it. It isn't exhilarating, and you know it.

Also, drop all that cold-bath nonsense. You never did it when you were a boy. Don't be a fool now. If you must take a bath (you don't really need to), take it warm. The pleasure of getting out of a cold bed and creeping into a hot bath beats a cold plunge to death. In any case, stop gassing about your tub and your "shower," as if you were the only man who ever washed.

So much for that point.

Next, take the question of germs and bacilli. Don't be scared of them. That's all. That's the whole thing, and if you once get on to that you never need to worry again.

If you see a bacilli, walk right up to it, and look it in the eye. If one flies into your room, strike at it with your hat or with a towel. Hit it as hard as you can between the neck and the thorax. It will soon get sick of that.

But as a matter of fact, a bacilli is perfectly quiet and harmless if you are not afraid of it. Speak to it. Call out to it to "lie down." It will understand. I had a bacilli once, called Fido, that would come and lie at my feet while I was working. I never knew a more affectionate companion, and when it was run over by an automobile, I buried it in the garden with genuine sorrow.

(I admit this is an exaggeration. I don't really remember its name; it may have been Robert.)

Understand that it is only a fad of modern medicine to say that cholera and typhoid and diphtheria are caused by bacilli and germs; nonsense. Cholera is caused by a frightful pain in the stomach, and diphtheria is caused by trying to cure a sore throat.

Now take the question of food.

Eat what you want. Eat lots of it. Yes, eat too much of it. Eat till you can just stagger across the room with it and prop it up against a sofa cushion. Eat everything that you like until you can't eat any more. The only test is, can you pay for it? If you can't pay for it, don't eat it. And listen—don't worry as to whether your food contains starch, or albumen, or gluten, or nitrogen. If you are damn fool enough to want these things, go and buy them and eat all you want of them. Go to a laundry and get a bag of starch, and eat your fill of it. Eat it, and take a good long drink of glue after it, and a spoonful of Portland cement. That will gluten you, good and solid.

If you like nitrogen, go and get a druggist to give you a canful of it at the soda counter, and let you sip it with a straw. Only don't think that you can mix all these things up with your food. There isn't any nitrogen or phosphorus or albumen in ordinary things to eat. In any decent household all that sort of stuff is washed out in the kitchen sink before the food is put on the table.

And just one word about fresh air and exercise. Don't bother with either of them. Get your room full of good air, then shut up the windows and keep it. It will keep for years. Anyway, don't keep using your lungs all the time. Let them rest. As for exercise, if you have to take it, take it and put up with it. But as long as you have the price of a hack and can hire other people to play baseball for you and run races and do gymnastics when you sit in the shade and smoke and watch them—great heavens, what more do you want?

HOW TO AVOID GETTING MARRIED

SOME years ago, when I was the Editor of a Correspondence Column, I used to receive heart-broken letters from young men asking for advice and sympathy. They found themselves the object of marked attentions from girls which they scarcely knew how to deal with. They did not wish to give pain or to seem indifferent to a love which they felt was as ardent as it was disinterested, and yet they felt that they could not bestow their hands where their hearts had not spoken. They wrote to me fully and frankly, and as one soul might write to another for relief. I accepted their confidences as under the pledge of a secrecy, never divulging their disclosures beyond the circulation of my newspapers, or giving any hint of their identity other than printing their names and addresses and their letters in full. But I may perhaps without dishonour reproduce one of these letters, and my answer to it, inasmuch as the date is now months ago, and the softening hand of Time has woven its roses—how shall I put it?—the mellow haze of reminiscences has—what I mean is that the young man has gone back to work and is all right again.

Here then is a letter from a young man whose name I must not reveal, but whom I will designate as D. F., and whose address I must not divulge, but will simply indicate as Q. Street, West.

"DEAR MR. LEACOCK,

"For some time past I have been the recipient of very marked attentions from a young lady. She has been calling at the house almost every evening, and has taken me out in her motor, and invited me to concerts and the theatre. On these latter occasions I have insisted on her taking my father with me, and have tried as far as possible to prevent her saying anything to me which would be unfit for father to hear. But my position has become a very difficult one. I do not think it right to accept her presents when I cannot feel that my heart is hers. Yesterday she sent to my house a beautiful bouquet of American Beauty roses addressed to me, and a magnificent bunch of Timothy Hay for father. I do not know what to say. Would it be right for father to keep all this valuable hay? I have confided fully in father, and we have discussed the question of presents. He thinks that there are some that we can keep with propriety, and others that a sense of delicacy forbids us to retain. He himself is going to sort out the presents into the two classes. He thinks that as far as he can see, the Hay is in class B. Meantime I write to you, as I understand that Miss Laura Jean Libby and Miss Beatrix Fairfax are on their vacation, and in any case a friend of mine who follows their writings closely tells me that they are always full.

"I enclose a dollar, because I do not think it right to ask you to give all your valuable time and your best thought without giving you back what it is worth."

On receipt of this I wrote back at once a private and confidential letter which I printed in the following edition of the paper.

"MY DEAR, DEAR BOY,

"Your letter has touched me. As soon as I opened it and saw the green and blue tint of the dollar bill which you had so daintily and prettily folded within the pages of your sweet letter, I knew that the note was from someone that I could learn to love, if our correspondence were to continue as it had begun. I took the dollar from your letter and kissed and fondled it a dozen times. Dear unknown boy! I shall always keep that dollar! No matter how much I may need it, or how many necessaries, yes, absolute necessities, of life I may be wanting, I shall always keep *that* dollar. Do you understand, dear? I shall keep it. I shall not spend it. As far as the *use* of it goes, it will be just as if you had not sent it. Even if you were to send me another dollar, I should still keep the first one, so that no matter how many you sent, the recollection of one first friendship would not be contaminated with mercenary considerations. When I say dollar, darling, of course an express order, or a postal note, or even stamps would be all the same. But in that case do not address me in care of this office, as I should not like to think of your pretty little letters lying round where others might handle them.

"But now I must stop chatting about myself, for I know that you cannot be interested in a simple old fogey such as I am. Let me talk to you about your letter and about the difficult question it raises for all marriageable young men.

"In the first place, let me tell you how glad I am that you confide in your father. Whatever happens, go at once to your father, put your arms about his neck, and have a good cry together. And you are right, too, about presents. It needs a wiser head than my poor perplexed boy to deal with them. Take them to your father to be sorted, or, if you feel that you must not overtax his love, address them to me in your own pretty hand.

"And now let us talk, dear, as one heart to another. Remember always that if a girl is to have your heart she must be worthy of you. When you look at your own bright innocent face in the mirror, resolve that you will give your hand to no girl who is not just as innocent as you are and no brighter than yourself. So that you must first find out how innocent she is. Ask her quietly and frankly—remember, dear, that the days of false modesty are passing away—whether she has ever been in jail. If she has not (and if *you* have not), then you know that you are dealing with a dear confiding girl who will make you a life mate. Then you must know, too, that her mind is worthy of your own. So many men to-day are led astray by the merely superficial graces and attractions of girls who in reality possess no mental equipment at all. Many a man is bitterly disillusioned after marriage when he realises that his wife cannot solve a quadratic equation, and that he is compelled to spend all his days with a woman who does not know that x squared plus $2xy$ plus y squared is the same thing, or, I think, nearly the same thing, as x plus y squared.

"Nor should the simple domestic virtues be neglected. If a girl desires to woo you, before allowing her to press her suit, ask her if she knows how to press yours. If she can, let her woo; if not, tell her to whoa. But I see I have written quite as much as I need for this column. Won't you write again, just as before, dear boy?

"STEPHEN LEACOCK."

HOW TO BE A DOCTOR

CERTAINLY the progress of science is a wonderful thing. One can't help feeling proud of it. I must admit that I do. Whenever I get talking to anyone—that is, to anyone who knows even less about it than I do—about the marvellous development of electricity, for instance, I feel as if I had been personally responsible for it. As for the linotype and the aeroplane and the vacuum house-cleaner, well, I am not sure that I didn't invent them myself. I believe that all generous-hearted men feel just the same way about it.

However, that is not the point I am intending to discuss. What I want to speak about is the progress of medicine. There, if you like, is something wonderful. Any lover of humanity (or of either sex of it) who looks back on the achievements of medical science must feel his heart glow and his right ventricle expand with the pericardiac stimulus of a permissible pride.

Just think of it. A hundred years ago there were no bacilli, no ptomaine poisoning, no diphtheria, and no appendicitis. Rabies was but little known, and only imperfectly developed. All of these things we owe to medical science. Even such things as psoriasis and parotitis and trypanosomiasis, which are now household names, were known only to the few, and were quite beyond the reach of the great mass of the people.

Or consider the advance of the science on its practical side. A hundred years ago it used to be supposed that fever could be cured by the letting of blood; now we know positively that it cannot. Even seventy years ago it was thought that fever was curable by the administration of sedative drugs; now we know that it isn't. For the matter of that, as recently as thirty years ago, doctors thought that they could heal a fever by means of low diet and the application of ice; now they are absolutely certain that they cannot. This instance shows the steady progress made in the treatment of fever. But there has been the same cheering advance all along the line. Take rheumatism. A few generations ago people with rheumatism used to have to carry round potatoes in their pockets as a means of cure. Now the doctors allow them to carry absolutely anything they like. They may go round with their pockets full of water-melons if they wish to. It makes no difference. Or take the treatment of epilepsy. It used to be supposed that the first thing to do in sudden attacks of this kind was to unfasten the patient's collar and let him breathe; at present, on the contrary, many doctors consider it better to button up the patient's collar and let him choke.

In only one respect has there been a decided lack of progress in the domain of medicine, that is in the time it takes to become a qualified practitioner. In the good old days a man was turned out thoroughly equipped after putting in two winter sessions at a college and spending his summers in running logs for a sawmill. Some of the students were turned out even sooner. Nowadays it takes anywhere from five to eight years to become a doctor. Of course, one is willing to grant that our young men are growing stupider and lazier every year. This fact will be corroborated at once by any man over fifty years of age. But even when this is said it seems odd that a man should study eight years now to learn what he used to acquire in eight months.

However, let that go. The point I want to develop is

that the modern doctor's business is an extremely simple one, which could be acquired in about two weeks. This is the way it is done.

The patient enters the consulting-room. "Doctor," he says, "I have a bad pain." "Where is it?" "Here." "Stand up," says the doctor, "and put your arms up above your head." Then the doctor goes behind the patient and strikes him a powerful blow in the back. "Do you feel that," he says. "I do," says the patient. Then the doctor turns suddenly and lets him have a left hook under the heart. "Can you feel that?" he says viciously, as the patient falls over on the sofa in a heap. "Get up," says the doctor, and counts ten. The patient rises. The doctor looks him over very carefully without speaking, and then suddenly fetches him a blow in the stomach that doubles him up speechless. The doctor walks over to the window and reads the morning papers for a while. Presently he turns and begins to mutter more to himself than to the patient. "Hum!" he says, "there's a slight anæsthesia of the tympanum." "Is that so?" says the patient, in an agony of fear. "What can I do about it, doctor?" "Well," says the doctor, "I want you to keep very quiet; you'll have to go to bed and stay there and keep quiet." In reality, of course, the doctor hasn't the least idea what is wrong with the man; but he *does* know that if he will go to bed and keep quiet, awfully quiet, he'll either get quietly well again or else die a quiet death. Meantime, if the doctor calls every morning and thumps and beats him, he can keep the patient submissive and perhaps force him to confess what is wrong with him.

"What about diet, doctor?" says the patient, completely cowed.

The answer to this question varies very much. It depends on how the doctor is feeling and whether it is long since he had a meal himself. If it is late in the morning and the doctor is ravenously hungry, he says: "Oh, eat plenty, don't be afraid of it; eat meat, vegetables, starch, glue, cement, anything you like." But if the doctor has just had lunch and his breathing is short-circuited with huckleberry-pie, he says very firmly: "No, I don't want you to eat anything at all: absolutely not a bite; it won't hurt you, a little self-denial in the matter of eating is the best thing in the world."

"And what about drinking?" Again the doctor's answer varies. He may say: "Oh, yes, you might drink a glass of lager now and then, or, if you prefer it, a gin and soda or a whisky and Apollinaris, and I think before going to bed I'd take a hot Scotch with a couple of lumps of white sugar and a bit of lemon-peel in it and a good grating of nutmeg on the top." The doctor says this with real feeling, and his eye glistens with the pure love of his profession. But if, on the other hand, the doctor has spent the night before at a little gathering of medical friends, he is very apt to forbid the patient to touch alcohol in any shape, and to dismiss the subject with great severity.

Of course, this treatment in and of itself would appear too transparent, and would fail to inspire the patient with a proper confidence. But nowadays this element is supplied by the work of the analytical laboratory. Whatever is wrong with the patient, the doctor insists on snipping off parts and pieces and extracts of him and sending them mysteriously away to be analysed. He cuts off a lock of the patient's hair, marks it, "Mr. Smith's Hair, October, 1910." Then he clips off the lower part of the ear, and wraps it in paper, and labels it, "Part of Mr. Smith's Ear, October, 1910." Then he looks the patient up and down, with the scissors in his hand, and if he sees any likely part of him he clips it off and wraps it up. Now this, oddly enough, is the very thing that fills the patient up with that sense of personal importance which is worth paying for. "Yes," says the bandaged patient, later in the day to a group of friends much impressed, "the doctor thinks there may be a slight anæsthesia of the prognosis, but he's sent my ear to New York and my appendix to Baltimore and a lock of my hair to the editors of all the medical journals, and meantime I am to keep very quiet and not exert myself beyond drinking a hot Scotch with lemon and nutmeg every half-hour." With that he sinks back faintly on his cushions, luxuriously happy.

And yet, isn't it funny?

You and I and the rest of us—even if we know all this—as soon as we have a pain within us, rush for a doctor as fast as a hack can take us. Yes, personally, I even prefer an ambulance with a bell on it. It's more soothing.

THE NEW FOOD

I SEE from the current columns of the daily press that "Professor Plumb, of the University of Chicago, has just invented a highly concentrated form of food. All the essential nutritive elements are put together in the form of pellets, each of which contains from one to two hundred times as much nourishment as an ounce of an ordinary article of diet. These pellets, diluted with water, will form all that is necessary to support life. The Professor looks forward confidently to revolutionising the present food system."

Now this kind of thing may be all very well in its way, but it is going to have its drawbacks as well. In the bright future anticipated by Professor Plumb, we can easily imagine such incidents as the following:

The smiling family were gathered round the hospitable board. The table was plenteously laid with a soup-plate in front of each beaming child, a bucket of hot water before the radiant mother, and at the head of the board the Christmas dinner of the happy home, warmly covered by a thimble and resting on a poker chip. The expectant whispers of the little ones were hushed as the father, rising from his chair, lifted the thimble and disclosed a small pill of concentrated nourishment on the chip before him. Christmas turkey, cranberry sauce, plum pudding, mince pie—it was all there, all jammed into that little pill and only waiting to expand. Then the father with deep reverence, and a devout eye alternating between the pill and heaven, lifted his voice in a benediction.

At this moment there was an agonised cry from the mother.

"Oh, Henry, quick! Baby has snatched the pill!" It was too true. Dear little Gustavus Adolphus, the golden-haired baby boy, had grabbed the whole Christmas dinner off the poker chip and bolted it. Three hundred and fifty pounds of concentrated nourishment passed down the œsophagus of the unthinking child.

"Clap him on the back!" cried the distracted mother. "Give him water!"

The idea was fatal. The water striking the pill caused it to expand. There was a dull rumbling sound and then, with an awful bang, Gustavus Adolphus exploded into fragments!

And when they gathered the little corpse together, the

baby lips were parted in a lingering smile that could only be worn by a child who had eaten thirteen Christmas dinners.

A NEW PATHOLOGY

IT has long been vaguely understood that the condition of a man's clothes has a certain effect upon the health of both body and mind. The well-known proverb, "Clothes make the man," has its origin in a general recognition of the powerful influence of the habiliments in their reaction upon the wearer. The same truth may be observed in the facts of everyday life. On the one hand we remark the bold carriage and mental vigour of a man attired in a new suit of clothes; on the other hand we note the melancholy features of him who is conscious of a posterior patch, or the haunted face of one suffering from internal loss of buttons. But while common observation thus gives us a certain familiarity with a few leading facts regarding the ailments and influence of clothes, no attempt has as yet been made to reduce our knowledge to a systematic form. At the same time the writer feels that a valuable addition might be made to the science of medicine in this direction. The numerous diseases which are caused by this fatal influence should receive a scientific analysis, and their treatment be included among the principles of the healing art. The diseases of the clothes may roughly be divided into medical cases and surgical cases, while these again fall into classes according to the particular garment through which the sufferer is attacked.

MEDICAL CASES

Probably no article of apparel is so liable to a diseased condition as the trousers. It may be well, therefore, to treat first those maladies to which they are subject.

I. Contractio Pantalunæ, or Shortening of the Legs of the Trousers, an extremely painful malady most frequently found in the growing youth. The first symptom is the appearance of a yawning space (lacuna) above the boots, accompanied by an acute sense of humiliation and a morbid anticipation of mockery. The application of treacle to the boots, although commonly recommended, may rightly be condemned as too drastic a remedy. The use of boots reaching to the knee, to be removed only at night, will afford immediate relief. In connection with Contractio is often found—

II. Inflatio Genu, or Bagging of the Knees of the Trousers, a disease whose symptoms are similar to those above. The patient shows an aversion to the standing posture, and, in acute cases, if the patient be compelled to stand, the head is bent and the eye fixed with painful rigidity upon the projecting blade formed at the knee of the trousers.

In both of the above diseases anything that can be done to free the mind of the patient from a morbid sense of his infirmity will do much to improve the general tone of the system.

III. Oases, or Patches, are liable to break out anywhere on the trousers, and range in degree of gravity from those of a trifling nature to those of a fatal character. The most distressing cases are those where the patch assumes a different colour from that of the trousers (dissimilitas coloris). In this instance the mind of the patient is found to be in a sadly aberrated condition. A speedy improvement may, however, be effected by cheerful society, books, flowers, and, above all, by a complete change.

IV. The overcoat is attacked by no serious disorders, except—

Phosphorescentia, or Glistening, a malady which indeed may often be observed to affect the whole system. It is caused by decay of tissue from old age and is generally aggravated by repeated brushing. A peculiar feature of the complaint is the lack of veracity on the part of the patient in reference to the cause of his uneasiness. Another invariable symptom is his aversion to outdoor exercise; under various pretexts, which it is the duty of his medical adviser firmly to combat, he will avoid even a gentle walk in the streets.

V. Of the waistcoat science recognises but one disease—

Porriggia, an affliction caused by repeated spilling of porridge. It is generally harmless, chiefly owing to the mental indifference of the patient. It can be successfully treated by repeated fomentations of benzine.

VI. Mortificatio Tilis, or Greenness of the Hat, is a disease often found in connection with Phosphorescentia (mentioned above), and characterised by the same aversion to outdoor life.

VII. Sterilitas, or Loss of Fur, is another disease of the hat, especially prevalent in winter. It is not accurately known whether this is caused by a falling out of the fur or by a cessation of growth. In all diseases of the hat the mind of the patient is greatly depressed and his countenance stamped with the deepest gloom. He is particularly sensitive in regard to questions as to the previous history of the hat.

Want of space precludes the mention of minor diseases, such as—

VIII. Odditus Soccorum, or Oddness of the Socks, a thing in itself trifling, but of an alarming nature if met in combination with Contractio Pantalunæ. Cases are found where the patient, possibly on the public platform or at a social gathering, is seized with a consciousness of the malady so suddenly as to render medical assistance futile.

SURGICAL CASES

It is impossible to mention more than a few of the most typical cases of diseases of this sort.

I. Explosio, or Loss of Buttons, is the commonest malady demanding surgical treatment. It consists of a succession of minor fractures, possibly internal, which at first excite no alarm. A vague sense of uneasiness is presently felt, which often leads the patient to seek relief in the string habit—a habit which, if unduly indulged in, may assume the proportions of a ruling passion. The use of sealing-wax, while admirable as a temporary remedy for Explosio, should never be allowed to gain a permanent hold upon the system. There is no doubt that a persistent indulgence in the string habit, or the constant use of sealing-wax, will result in—

II. Fractura Suspendorum, or Snapping of the Braces, which amounts to a general collapse of the system. The patient is usually seized with a severe attack of Explosio, followed by a sudden sinking feeling and sense of loss. A sound constitution may rally from the shock, but a system undermined by the string habit invariably succumbs.

III. Sectura Pantalunæ, or Ripping of the Trousers, is generally caused by sitting upon warm beeswax or leaning against a hook. In the case of the very young it is not unfrequently accompanied by a distressing suppuration of the shirt. This, however, is not remarked in adults. The malady is rather mental than bodily, the mind of the patient being racked by a keen sense of indignity and a feeling of unworthiness. The only treatment is immediate isolation, with a careful stitching of the affected part.

In conclusion, it may be stated that at the first symptom of disease the patient should not hesitate to put himself in the hands of a professional tailor. In so brief a compass as the present article the discussion has of necessity been rather suggestive than exhaustive. Much yet remains to be done, and the subject opens wide to the inquiring eye. The writer will, however, feel amply satisfied if this brief outline may help to direct the attention of medical men to what is yet an unexplored field.

THE POET ANSWERED

DEAR SIR:

In answer to your repeated questions and requests which have appeared for some years past in the columns of the rural press, I beg to submit the following solutions of your chief difficulties:—

Topic I.—You frequently ask, where are the friends of your childhood, and urge that they shall be brought back to you. As far as I am able to learn, those of your friends who are not in jail are still right there in your native village. You point out that they were wont to share your gambols. If so, you are certainly entitled to have theirs now.

Topic II.—You have taken occasion to say:

"Give me not silk, nor rich attire,
Nor gold, nor jewels rare."

But, my dear fellow, this is preposterous. Why, these are the very things I had bought for you. If you won't take any of these, I shall have to give you factory cotton and cordwood.

Topic III.—You also ask, "How fares my love across the sea?" Intermediate, I presume. She would hardly travel steerage.

Topic IV.—"Why was I born? Why should I breathe?" Here I quite agree with you. I don't think you ought to breathe.

Topic V.—You demand that I shall show you the man whose soul is dead and then mark him. I am awfully sorry; the man was around here all day yesterday, and if I had only known I could easily have marked him so that we could pick him out again.

Topic VI.—I notice that you frequently say, "Oh, for the sky of your native land." Oh, for it, by all means, if you wish. But remember that you already owe for a great deal.

Topic VII.—On more than one occasion you wish to be informed, "What boots it, that you idly dream?" Nothing boots it at present—a fact, sir, which ought to afford you the highest gratification.

THE FORCE OF STATISTICS

THEY were sitting on a seat of the car, immediately in front of me. I was consequently able to hear all that they were saying. They were evidently strangers who had dropped into a conversation. They both had the air of men who considered themselves profoundly interesting as minds. It was plain that each laboured under the impression that he was a ripe thinker.

One had just been reading a book which lay in his lap.

"I've been reading some very interesting statistics," he was saying to the other thinker.

"Ah, statistics!" said the other; "wonderful things, sir, statistics; very fond of them myself."

"I find, for instance," the first man went on, "that a drop of water is filled with little . . . with little . . . I forget just what you call them . . . little—er—things, every cubic inch containing—er—containing . . . let me see . . ."

"Say a million," said the other thinker, encouragingly.

"Yes, a million, or possibly a billion . . . but at any rate, ever so many of them."

"Is it possible?" said the other. "But really, you know, there are wonderful things in the world. Now, coal . . . take coal. . . ."

"Very good," said his friend, "let us take coal," settling back in his seat with the air of an intellect about to feed itself.

"Do you know that every ton of coal burnt in an engine will drag a train of cars as long as . . . I forget the exact length, but say a train of cars of such and such a length, and weighing, say so much . . . from . . . from . . . hum! for the moment the exact distance escapes me . . . drag it from . . ."

"From here to the moon," suggested the other.

"Ah, very likely; yes, from here to the moon. Wonderful, isn't it?"

"But the most stupendous calculation of all, sir, is in regard to the distance from the earth to the sun. Positively, sir, a cannon-ball—er—fired at the sun . . ."

"Fired at the sun," nodded the other, approvingly, as if he had often seen it done.

"And travelling at the rate of . . . of . . ."

"Of three cents a mile," hinted the listener.

"No, no, you misunderstand me—but travelling at a fearful rate, simply fearful, sir, would take a hundred million—no, a hundred billion—in short would take a scandalously long time in getting there——"

At this point I could stand no more. I interrupted—"Provided it were fired from Philadelphia," I said, and passed into the smoking-car.

MEN WHO HAVE SHAVED ME

A BARBER is by nature and inclination a sport. He can tell you at what exact hour the ball game of the day is to begin, can foretell its issue without losing a stroke of the razor, and can explain the points of inferiority of all the players, as compared with better men that he has personally seen elsewhere, with the nicety of a professional. He can do all this, and then stuff the customer's mouth with a soap-brush, and leave him while he goes to the other end of the shop to make a side bet with one of the other barbers on the outcome of the Autumn Handicap. In the barber-shops they knew the result of the Jeffries-Johnson prize fight long before it happened. It is on information of this kind that they make their living. The performance of shaving is only incidental to it. Their real vocation in life is imparting information. To the barber the outside world is made up of customers, who are to be thrown into chairs, strapped, manacled, gagged with soap, and then given such necessary information on the athletic events of the moment as will carry them through the business hours of the day without open disgrace.

As soon as the barber has properly filled up the customer with information of this sort, he rapidly removes his whiskers as a sign that the man is now fit to talk to, and lets him out of the chair.

The public has grown to understand the situation. Every reasonable business man is willing to sit and wait half an hour for a shave which he could give himself in three minutes, because he knows that if he goes down town without understanding exactly why Chicago lost two games straight he will appear an ignoramus.

At times, of course, the barber prefers to test his customer, with a question or two. He gets him pinned in the chair, with his head well back, covers the customer's face with soap, and then planting his knee on his chest and holding his hand firmly across the customer's mouth, to prevent all utterance and to force him to swallow the soap, he asks: "Well, what did you think of the Detroit-St. Louis game yesterday?" This is not really meant for a question at all. It is only equivalent to saying: "Now, you poor fool, I'll bet you don't know anything about the great events of your country at all." There is a gurgle in the customer's throat as if he were trying to answer, and his eyes are seen to move sideways, but the barber merely thrusts the soapbrush into each eye, and if any motion still persists, he breathes gin and peppermint over the face, till all sign of life is extinct. Then he talks the game over in detail with the barber at the next chair, each leaning across an inanimate thing extended under steaming towels that was once a man.

To know all these things barbers have to be highly educated. It is true that some of the greatest barbers that have ever lived have begun as uneducated, illiterate men, and by sheer energy and indomitable industry have forced their way to the front. But these are exceptions. To succeed nowadays it is practically necessary to be a college graduate. As the courses at Harvard and Yale have been found too superficial, there are now established regular Barbers' Colleges, where a bright young man can learn as much in three weeks as he would be likely to know after three years at Harvard. The courses at these colleges cover such things as (1) PHYSIOLOGY, including *Hair and its Destruction, The Origin and Growth of Whiskers, Soap in its Relation to Eyesight;* (2) CHEMISTRY, including lectures on Florida Water; and How to Make it out of Sardine Oil; (3) PRACTICAL ANATOMY, including *The Scalp and How to Lift it, The Ears and How to Remove them,* and, as the Major Course for advanced students, The Veins of the Face and how to open and close them at will by the use of alum.

The education of the customer is, as I have said, the chief part of the barber's vocation. But it must be remembered that the incidental function of removing his whiskers in order to mark him as a well-informed man is also of importance, and demands long practice and great natural aptitude. In the barbers' shops of modern cities shaving has been brought to a high degree of perfection. A good barber is not content to remove the whiskers of his client directly and immediately. He prefers to cook him first. He does this by immersing the head in hot water and covering the victim's face with steaming towels until he has him boiled to a nice pink. From time to time the barber removes the towels and looks at the face to see if it is yet boiled pink enough for his satisfaction. If it is not, he replaces the towels again and jams them down firmly with his hand until the cooking is finished. The final result, however, amply justifies this trouble, and the well-boiled customer only needs the addition of a few vegetables on the side to present an extremely appetizing appearance.

During the process of the shave, it is customary for the barber to apply the particular kind of mental torture known as the third degree. This is done by terrorising the patient as to the very evident and proximate loss of all his hair and whiskers, which the barber is enabled by his experience to foretell. "Your hair," he says, very sadly and sympathetically, "is all falling out. Better let me give you a shampoo?" "No." "Let me singe your hair to close up the follicles?" "No." "Let me plug up the ends of your hair with sealing-wax, it's the only thing that will save it for you?" "No." "Let me rub an egg on your scalp?" "No." "Let me squirt a lemon on your eyebrows?" "No."

The barber sees that he is dealing with a man of determination, and he warms to his task. He bends low and whispers into the prostrate ear: "You've got a good many grey hairs coming in; better let me give you an application of Hairocene, only cost you half a dollar?" "No." "Your face," he whispers again, with a soft, caressing voice, "is all covered with wrinkles; better let me rub some of this Rejuvenator into the face."

This process is continued until one of two things happens. Either the customer is obdurate, and staggers to his feet at last and gropes his way out of the shop with the knowledge that he is a wrinkled, prematurely senile man, whose wicked life is stamped upon his face, and whose unstopped hair-ends and failing follicles menace him with the certainty of complete baldness within twenty-four hours—or else, as in nearly all instances, he succumbs. In the latter case, immediately on his saying "yes" there is a shout of exultation from the barber, a roar of steaming water, and within a moment two barbers have grabbed him by the feet and thrown him under the tap, and, in spite of his struggles, are giving him the Hydro-magnetic treatment. When he emerges from their hands, he steps out of the shop looking as if he had been varnished.

But even the application of the Hydro-magnetic and the Rejuvenator do not by any means exhaust the resources of the up-to-date barber. He prefers to perform on the customer a whole variety of subsidiary services not directly connected with shaving, but carried on during the process of the shave.

In a good, up-to-date shop, while one man is shaving the customer, others black his boots, brush his clothes, darn his socks, point his nails, enamel his teeth, polish his eyes, and alter the shape of any of his joints which they think unsightly. During this operation they often stand seven deep round a customer, fighting for a chance to get at him.

All of these remarks apply to barber-shops in the city, and not to country places. In the country there is only one barber and one customer at a time. The thing assumes the aspect of a straight-out, rough-and-tumble, catch-as-catch-can fight, with a few spectators sitting round the shop to see fair play. In the city they can shave a man without removing any of his clothes. But in the country, where the customer insists on getting the full value for his money, they remove the collar and necktie, the coat and the waistcoat, and, for a really good shave and hair-cut, the customer is stripped to the waist. The barber can then take a rush at him from the other side of the room, and drive the clippers up the full length of the spine, so as to come at the heavier hair on the back of the head with the impact of a lawn-mower driven into long grass.

GETTING THE THREAD OF IT

HAVE you ever had a man try to explain to you what happened in a book as far as he has read? It is a most instructive thing. Sinclair, the man who shares my rooms with me, made such an attempt the other night. I had come in cold and tired from a walk and found him full of excitement, with a bulky magazine in one hand and a paper-cutter gripped in the other.

"Say, here's a grand story," he burst out as soon as I came in; "it's great! most fascinating thing I ever read. Wait till I read you some of it. I'll just tell you what has happened up to where I am—you'll easily catch the thread of it—and then we'll finish it together."

I wasn't feeling in a very responsive mood, but I saw no way to stop him, so I merely said, "All right, throw me your thread, I'll catch it."

"Well," Sinclair began with great animation, "this count gets this letter . . ."

"Hold on," I interrupted, "what count gets what letter?"

"Oh, the count it's about, you know. He gets this letter from this Porphirio . . ."

"From which Porphirio?"

"Why, Porphirio sent the letter, don't you see, he sent it," Sinclair exclaimed a little impatiently—"sent it through Demonio and told him to watch for him with him, and kill him when he got him."

"Oh, see here!" I broke in, "who is to meet who, and who is to get stabbed?"

"They're going to stab Demonio."

"And who brought the letter?"

"Demonio."

"Well, now, Demonio must be a clam! What did he bring it for?"

"Oh, but he don't know what's in it, that's just the slick part of it," and Sinclair began to snigger to himself at the thought of it. "You see, this Carlo Carlotti the Condottiere . . ."

"Stop right there," I said. "What's a Condottiere?"

"It's a sort of brigand. He, you understand, was in league with this Fra Fraliccolo . . ."

A suspicion flashed across my mind. "Look here," I said firmly, "if the scene of this story is laid in the Highlands, I refuse to listen to it. Call it off."

"No, no," Sinclair answered quickly, "that's all right. It's laid in Italy . . . time of Pius the something. He comes in—say, but he's great! so darned crafty. It's him, you know, that persuades this Franciscan . . ."

"Pause," I said, "what Franciscan?"

"Fra Fraliccolo, of course," Sinclair said snappishly. "You see, Pio tries to . . ."

"Whoa!" I said, "who is Pio?"

"Oh, hang it all, Pio is Italian, it's short for Pius. He tries to get Fra Fraliccolo and Carlo Carlotti the Condottiere to steal the document from . . . let me see, what was he called? . . . Oh, yes . . . from the Dog of Venice, so that . . . or . . . no, hang it, you put me out, that's all wrong. It's the other way round. Pio wasn't clever at all; he's a regular darned fool. It's the Dog that's crafty. By Jove, he's fine," Sinclair went on, warming up to enthusiasm again, "he just does anything he wants. He makes this Demonio (Demonio is one of those hirelings, you know, he's the tool of the Dog) . . . makes him steal the document off Porphirio, and . . ."

"But how does he get him to do that?" I asked.

"Oh, the Dog has Demonio pretty well under his thumb, so he makes Demonio scheme round till he gets old Pio—er—gets him under his thumb, and then, of course, Pio thinks that Porphirio—I mean he thinks that he has Porphirio—er—has him under his thumb."

"Half a minute, Sinclair," I said, "who did you say was under the Dog's thumb?"

"Demonio."

"Thanks. I was mixed in the thumbs. Go on."

"Well, just when things are like this . . ."

"Like what?"

"Like I said."

"All right."

"Who should turn up and thwart the whole scheme, but this Signorina Tarara in her domino . . ."

"Hully Gee!" I said, "you make my head ache. What the deuce does she come in her domino for?"

"Why, to thwart it."

"To thwart what?"

"Thwart the whole darned thing," Sinclair exclaimed emphatically.

"But can't she thwart it without her domino?"

"I should think not! You see, if it hadn't been for the domino, the Dog would have spotted her quick as a wink. Only when he sees her in the domino with this rose in her hair, he thinks she must be Lucia dell' Esterolla."

"Say, he fools himself, doesn't he? Who's this last girl?"

"Lucia? Oh, she's great!" Sinclair said. "She's one of those Southern natures, you know, full of—er—full of . . ."

"Full of fun," I suggested.

"Oh, hang it all, don't make fun of it! Well, anyhow, she's sister, you understand, to the Contessa Carantarata, and that's why Fra Fraliccolo, or . . . hold on, that's not it, no, no, she's not sister to anybody. She's cousin, that's it; or, anyway, she thinks she is cousin to Fra Fraliccolo himself, and that's why Pio tries to stab Fra Fraliccolo."

"Oh, yes," I assented, "naturally he would."

"Ah," Sinclair said hopefully, getting his paper-cutter ready to cut the next pages, "you begin to get the thread now, don't you?"

"Oh, fine!" I said. "The people in it are the Dog and Pio, and Carlo Carlotti the Condottiere, and those others that we spoke of."

"That's right," Sinclair said. "Of course, there are more still that I can tell you about if . . ."

"Oh, never mind," I said, "I'll work along with those, they're a pretty representative crowd. Then Porphirio is under Pio's thumb, and Pio is under Demonio's thumb, and the Dog is crafty, and Lucia is full of something all the time. Oh, I've got a mighty clear idea of it," I concluded bitterly.

"Oh, you've got it," Sinclair said, "I knew you'd like it. Now we'll go on. I'll just finish to the bottom of my page and then I'll go on aloud."

He ran his eyes rapidly over the lines till he came to the bottom of the page, then he cut the leaves and turned over. I saw his eye rest on the half-dozen lines that confronted him on the next page with an expression of utter consternation.

"Well, I will be cursed!" he said at length.

"What's the matter?" I said gently, with a great joy at my heart.

"This infernal thing's a serial," he gasped, as he pointed at the words *To be continued*, "and that's all there is in this number."

TELLING HIS FAULTS

"OH, do, Mr. Sapling," said the beautiful girl at the summer hotel, "do let me read the palm of your hand! I can tell you all your faults."

Mr. Sapling gave an inarticulate gurgle and a roseate flush swept over his countenance as he surrendered his palm to the grasp of the fair enchantress.

"Oh, you're just full of faults, just full of them, Mr. Sapling!" she cried.

Mr. Sapling looked it.

"To begin with," said the beautiful girl, slowly and reflectingly, "you are dreadfully cynical: you hardly believe in anything at all, and you've utterly no faith in us poor women."

The feeble smile that had hitherto kindled the features of Mr. Sapling into a ray of chastened imbecility, was distorted in an effort at cynicism.

"Then your next fault is that you are too determined; much too determined. When once you have set your will on any object, you crush every obstacle under your feet."

Mr. Sapling looked meekly down at his tennis shoes, but began to feel calmer, more lifted up. Perhaps he had been all these things without knowing it.

"Then you are cold and sarcastic."

Mr. Sapling attempted to look cold and sarcastic. He succeeded in a rude leer.

"And you're horribly world-weary, you care for nothing. You have drained philosophy to the dregs, and scoff at everything."

Mr. Sapling's inner feeling was that from now on he would simply scoff and scoff and scoff.

"Your only redeeming quality is that you are generous. You have tried to kill even this, but cannot. Yes," concluded the beautiful girl, "those are your faults, generous still, but cold, cynical and relentless. Good night, Mr. Sapling."

And resisting all entreaties the beautiful girl passed from the verandah of the hotel and vanished.

And when later in the evening the brother of the beautiful girl borrowed Mr. Sapling's tennis racket, and his bicycle for a fortnight, and the father of the beautiful girl got Sapling to endorse his note for a couple of hundreds, and her uncle Zephas borrowed his bedroom candle and used his razor to cut up a plug of tobacco, Mr. Sapling felt proud to be acquainted with the family.

WINTER PASTIMES

It is in the depth of winter, when the intense cold renders it desirable to stay at home, that the really Pleasant Family is wont to serve invitations upon a few friends to spend a Quiet Evening.

It is at these gatherings that that gay thing, the indoor winter game, becomes rampant. It is there that the old euchre deck and the staring domino become fair and beautiful things; that the rattle of the Loto counter rejoices the heart, that the old riddle feels the sap stirring in its limbs again, and the amusing spilikin completes the mental ruin of the jaded guest. Then does the Jolly Maiden Aunt propound the query: What is the difference between an elephant and a silk hat? Or declare that her first is a vowel, her second a preposition, and her third an archipelago. It is to crown such a quiet evening, and to give the finishing stroke to those of the visitors who have not escaped early, with a fierce purpose of getting at the saloons before they have time to close, that the indoor game or family reservoir of fun is dragged from its long sleep. It is spread out upon the table. Its paper of directions is unfolded. Its cards, its counters, its pointers and its markers are distributed around the table, and the visitor forces a look of reckless pleasure upon his face. Then the "few simple directions" are read aloud by the Jolly Aunt, instructing each player to challenge the player holding the golden letter corresponding to the digit next in order, to name a dead author beginning with *X*, failing which the player must declare himself in fault, and pay the forfeit of handing over to the Jolly Aunt his gold watch and all his money, or having a hot plate put down his neck.

With a view to bringing some relief to the guests at entertainments of this kind, I have endeavoured to construct one or two little winter pastimes of a novel character. They are quite inexpensive, and as they need no background of higher arithmetic or ancient history, they are within reach of the humblest intellect. Here is one of them. It is called Indoor Football, or Football without a Ball.

In this game any number of players, from fifteen to thirty, seat themselves in a heap on any one player, usually the player next to the dealer. They then challenge him to get up, while one player stands with a stop-watch in his hand and counts forty seconds. Should the first player fail to rise before forty seconds are counted, the player with the watch declares him suffocated. This is called a "Down" and counts one. The player who was the Down is then leant against the wall; his wind is supposed to be squeezed out. The player called the referee then blows a whistle and the players select another player and score a down off him. While the player is supposed to be down, all the rest must remain seated as before, and not rise from him until the referee by counting forty and blowing his whistle announces that in his opinion the other player is stifled. He is then leant against the wall beside the first player. When the whistle again blows the player nearest the referee strikes him behind the right ear. This is a "Touch," and counts two.

It is impossible, of course, to give all the rules in detail. I might add, however, that while it counts *two* to strike the referee, to kick him counts *three*. To break his arm or leg counts *four*, and to kill him outright is called *Grand Slam* and counts one game.

Here is another little thing that I have worked out, which is superior to parlour games in that it combines their intense excitement with sound out-of-door exercise.

It is easily comprehended, and can be played by any number of players, old and young. It requires no other apparatus than a trolley car ot the ordinary type, a mile or two of track, and a few thousand volts of electricity. It is called:

The Suburban Trolley Car
A Holiday Game for Old and Young

The chief part in the game is taken by two players who station themselves one at each end of the car, and who adopt some distinctive costumes to indicate that they are "it." The other players occupy the body of the car, or take up their position at intervals along the track.

The object of each player should be to enter the car as stealthily as possible in such a way as to escape the notice of the players in distinctive dress. Should he fail to do this he must pay the philopena or forfeit. Of these there àre two: philopena No. 1, the payment of five cents, and philopena No. 2, being thrown off the car by the neck. Each player may elect which philopena he will pay. Any player who escapes paying the philopena scores one.

The players who are in the car may elect to adopt a standing attitude, or to seat themselves, but no player may seat himself in the lap of another without the second player's consent. The object of those who elect to remain standing is to place their feet upon the toes of those who sit; when they do this they score. The object of those who elect to sit is to elude the feet of the standing players. Much merriment is thus occasioned.

The player in distinctive costume at the front of the

car controls a crank, by means of which he is enabled to bring the car to a sudden stop, or to cause it to plunge violently forward. His aim in so doing is to cause all the standing players to fall over backward. Every time he does this he scores. For this purpose he is generally in collusion with the other player in distinctive costume, whose business it is to let him know by a series of bells and signals when the players are not looking, and can be easily thrown down. A sharp fall of this sort gives rise to no end of banter and good-natured drollery, directed against the two players who are "it."

Should a player who is thus thrown backward save himself from falling by sitting down in the lap of a female player, he scores one. Any player who scores in this manner is entitled to remain seated while he may count six, after which he must remove himself or pay philopena No. 2.

Should the player who controls the crank perceive a player upon the street desirous of joining in the game by entering the car, his object should be: primo, to run over him and kill him; secundo, to kill him by any other means in his power; tertio, to let him into the car, but to exact the usual philopena.

Should a player, in thus attempting to get on the car from without, become entangled in the machinery, the player controlling the crank shouts "huff!" and the car is supposed to pass over him. All within the car score one.

A fine spice of the ludicrous may be added to the game by each player pretending that he has a destination or stopping-place, where he would wish to alight. It now becomes the aim of the two players who are "it" to carry him past his point. A player who is thus carried beyond his imaginary stopping-place must feign a violent passion, and imitate angry gesticulations. He may, in addition, feign a great age or a painful infirmity, which will be found to occasion the most convulsive fun for the other players in the game.

These are the main outlines of this most amusing pastime. Many other agreeable features may, of course, be readily introduced by persons of humour and imagination.

NUMBER FIFTY-SIX

WHAT I narrate was told me one winter's evening by my friend Ah-Yen in the little room behind his laundry. Ah-Yen is a quiet little celestial with a grave and thoughtful face, and that melancholy contemplative disposition so often noticed in his countrymen. Between myself and Ah-Yen there exists a friendship of some years' standing, and we spend many a long evening in the dimly lighted room behind his shop, smoking a dreamy pipe together and plunged in silent meditation. I am chiefly attracted to my friend by the highly imaginative cast of his mind, which is, I believe, a trait of the Eastern character and which enables him to forget to a great extent the sordid cares of his calling in an inner life of his own creation. Of the keen, analytical side of his mind, I was in entire ignorance until the evening of which I write.

The room where we sat was small and dingy, with but little furniture except our chairs and the little table at which we filled and arranged our pipes, and was lighted only by a tallow candle. There were a few pictures on the walls, for the most part rude prints cut from the columns of the daily press and pasted up to hide the bareness of the room. Only one picture was in any way noticeable, a portrait admirably executed in pen and ink. The face was that of a young man, a very beautiful face, but one of infinite sadness. I had long been aware, although I know not how, that Ah-Yen had met with a great sorrow, and had in some way connected the fact with this portrait. I had always refrained, however, from asking him about it, and it was not until the evening in question that I knew its history.

We had been smoking in silence for some time when Ah-Yen spoke. My friend is a man of culture and wide reading, and his English is consequently perfect in its construction; his speech is, of course, marked by the lingering liquid accent of his country which I will not attempt to reproduce.

"I see," he said, "that you have been examining the portrait of my unhappy friend, Fifty-Six. I have never yet told you of my bereavement, but as to-night is the anniversary of his death, I would fain speak of him for a while."

Ah-Yen paused; I lighted my pipe afresh, and nodded to him to show that I was listening.

"I do not know," he went on, "at what precise time Fifty-Six came into my life. I could indeed find it out by examining my books, but I have never troubled to do so. Naturally I took no more interest in him at first than in any other of my customers—less, perhaps, since he never in the course of our connection brought his clothes to me himself but always sent them by a boy. When I presently perceived that he was becoming one of my regular customers, I allotted to him his number, Fifty-Six, and began to speculate as to who and what he was. Before long I had reached several conclusions in regard to my unknown client. The quality of his linen showed me that, if not rich, he was at any rate fairly well off. I could see that he was a young man of regular Christian life, who went out into society to a certain extent; this I could tell from his sending the same number of articles to the laundry, from his washing always coming on Saturday night, and from the fact that he wore a dress shirt about once a week. In disposition he was a modest, unassuming fellow, for his collars were only two inches high."

I stared at Ah-Yen in some amazement, the recent publications of a favourite novelist had rendered me familiar with this process of analytical reasoning, but I was prepared for no such revelations from my Eastern friend.

"When I first knew him," Ah-Yen went on, "Fifty-Six was a student at the university. This, of course, I did not know for some time. I inferred it, however, in the course of time, from his absence from town during the four summer months, and from the fact that during the time of the university examinations the cuffs of his shirts came to me covered with dates, formulas, and propositions in geometry. I followed him with no little interest through his university career. During the four years which it lasted, I washed for him every week; my regular connection with him and the insight which my observation gave me into the lovable character of the man, deepened my first esteem into a profound affection and I became most anxious for his success. I helped him at each succeeding examination, as far as lay in my power, by starching his shirts half-way to the elbow, so as to leave him as much room as possible for annotations. My anxiety during the strain of his final examination I will not attempt to describe. That Fifty-Six was undergoing the great crisis of his academic career, I could infer from the state of his handkerchiefs which, in apparent unconsciousness, he used as pen-wipers during the final test.

His conduct throughout the examination bore witness to the moral development which had taken place in his character during his career as an undergraduate; for the notes upon his cuffs which had been so copious at his earlier examinations were limited now to a few hints, and these upon topics so intricate as to defy an ordinary memory. It was with a thrill of joy that I at last received in his laundry bundle one Saturday early in June, a ruffled dress shirt, the bosom of which was thickly spattered with the spillings of the wine-cup, and realised that Fifty-Six had banqueted as a Bachelor of Arts.

"In the following winter the habit of wiping his pen upon his handkerchief, which I had remarked during his final examination, became chronic with him, and I knew that he had entered upon the study of law. He worked hard during that year, and dress shirts almost disappeared from his weekly bundle. It was in the following winter, the second year of his legal studies, that the tragedy of his life began. I became aware that a change had come over his laundry; from one, or at most two a week, his dress shirts rose to four, and silk handkerchiefs began to replace his linen ones. It dawned upon me that Fifty-Six was abandoning the rigorous tenor of his student life and was going into society. I presently perceived something more; Fifty-Six was in love. It was soon impossible to doubt it. He was wearing seven shirts a week; linen handkerchiefs disappeared from his laundry; his collars rose from two inches to two and a quarter, and finally to two and a half. I have in my possession one of his laundry lists of that period; a glance at it will show the scrupulous care which he bestowed upon his person. Well do I remember the dawning hopes of those days, alternating with the gloomiest despair. Each Saturday I opened his bundle with a trembling eagerness to catch the first signs of a return of his love. I helped my friend in every way that I could. His shirts and collars were masterpieces of my art, though my hand often shook with agitation as I applied the starch. She was a brave noble girl, that I knew; her influence was elevating the whole nature of Fifty-Six; until now he had had in his possession a certain number of detached cuffs and false shirt-fronts. These he discarded now—at first the false shirt-fronts, scorning the very idea of fraud, and after a time, in his enthusiasm, abandoning even the cuffs. I cannot look back upon those bright happy days of courtship without a sigh.

"The happiness of Fifty-Six seemed to enter into and fill my whole life. I lived but from Saturday to Saturday. The appearance of false shirt-fronts would cast me to the lowest depths of despair; their absence raised me to a pinnacle of hope. It was not till winter softened into spring that Fifty-Six nerved himself to learn his fate. One Saturday he sent me a new white waistcoat, a garment which had hitherto been shunned by his modest nature, to prepare for his use. I bestowed upon it all the resources of my art; I read his purpose in it. On the Saturday following it was returned to me and, with tears of joy, I marked where a warm little hand had rested fondly on the right shoulder, and knew that Fifty-Six was the accepted lover of his sweetheart."

Ah-Yen paused and sat for some time silent; his pipe had sputtered out and lay cold in the hollow of his hand; his eye was fixed upon the wall where the light and shadows shifted in the dull flickering of the candle. At last he spoke again:

"I will not dwell upon the happy days that ensued—days of gaudy summer neckties and white waistcoats, of spotless shirts and lofty collars worn but a single day by the fastidious lover. Our happiness seemed complete and I asked no more from fate. Alas! it was not destined to continue! When the bright days of summer were fading into autumn, I was grieved to notice an occasional quarrel—only four shirts instead of seven, or the reappearance of the abandoned cuffs and shirt-fronts. Reconciliations followed, with tears of penitence upon the shoulder of the white waistcoat, and the seven shirts came back. But the quarrels grew more frequent and there came at times stormy scenes of passionate emotion that left a track of broken buttons down the waistcoat. The shirts went slowly down to three, then fell to two, and the collars of my unhappy friend subsided to an inch and three-quarters. In vain I lavished my utmost care upon Fifty-Six. It seemed to my tortured mind that the gloss upon his shirts and collars would have melted a heart of stone. Alas! my every effort at reconciliation seemed to fail. An awful month passed; the false fronts and detached cuffs were all back again; the unhappy lover seemed to glory in their perfidy. At last, one gloomy evening, I found on opening his bundle that he had bought a stock of celluloids, and my heart told me that she had abandoned him for ever. Of what my poor friend suffered at this time, I can give you no idea; suffice it to say that he passed from celluloid to a blue flannel shirt and from blue to grey. The sight of a red cotton handkerchief in his wash at length warned me that his disappointed love had unhinged his mind, and I feared the worst. Then came an agonising interval of three weeks during which he sent me nothing, and after that came the last parcel that I ever received from him—an enormous bundle that seemed to contain all his effects. In this, to my horror, I discovered one shirt the breast of which was stained a deep crimson with his blood. and pierced by a ragged hole that showed where a bullet had singed through into his heart.

"A fortnight before, I remembered having heard the street boys crying the news of an appalling suicide, and I know now that it must have been he. After the first shock of my grief had passed, I sought to keep him in my memory by drawing the portrait which hangs beside you. I have some skill in the art, and I feel assured that I have caught the expression of his face. The picture is, of course, an ideal one, for, as you know, I never saw Fifty-Six."

The bell on the door of the outer shop tinkled at the entrance of a customer. Ah-Yen rose with that air of quiet resignation that habitually marked his demeanour, and remained for some time in the shop. When he returned he seemed in no mood to continue speaking of his lost friend. I left him soon after and walked sorrowfully home to my lodgings. On my way I mused much upon my little Eastern friend and the sympathetic grasp of his imagination. But a burden lay heavy on my heart —something I would fain have told him but which I could not bear to mention. I could not find it in my heart to shatter the airy castle of his fancy. For my life has been secluded and lonely and I have known no love like that of my ideal friend. Yet I have a haunting recollection of a certain huge bundle of washing that I sent to him about a year ago. I had been absent from town for three weeks and my laundry was much larger than usual in consequence. And if I mistake not there was in the bundle a tattered shirt that had been grievously stained by the breaking of a bottle of red ink in my portmanteau, and burnt in one place where an ash fell from my cigar as I made up the bundle. Of all this I cannot feel absolutely certain, yet I know at least that until a year ago, when I transferred my custom to a more modern establishment, my laundry number with Ah-Yen was Fifty-Six.

ARISTOCRATIC EDUCATION

HOUSE OF LORDS, Jan. 25, 1920—The House of Lords commenced to-day in Committee the consideration of Clause No. 52,000 of the Education Bill, dealing with the teaching of Geometry in schools.

The Leader of the Government in presenting the clause urged upon their Lordships the need of conciliation. The Bill, he said, had now been before their Lordships for sixteen years. The Government had made every concession. They had accepted all the amendments of their Lordships on the opposite side in regard to the original provisions of the Bill. They had consented also to insert in the Bill a detailed programme of studies of which the present clause, enunciating the fifth proposition of Euclid, was a part. He would therefore ask their Lordships to accept the clause drafted as follows:

"The angles at the base of an isosceles triangle are equal, and if the equal sides of the triangle are produced, the exterior angles will also be equal."

He would hasten to add that the Government had no intention of producing the sides. Contingencies might arise to render such a course necessary, but in that case their Lordships would receive an early intimation of the fact.

The Archbishop of Canterbury spoke against the

clause. He considered it, in its present form, too secular. He should wish to amend the clause so as to make it read:

"The angles at the base of an isosceles triangle are, in every Christian community, equal, and if the sides be produced by a member of a Christian congregation, the exterior angles will be equal."

He was aware, he continued, that the angles at the base of an isosceles triangle are extremely equal, but he must remind the Government that the Church had been aware of this for several years past. He was willing also to admit that the opposite sides and ends of a parallelogram are equal, but he thought that such an admission should be coupled with a distinct recognition of the existence of a Supreme Being.

The Leader of the Government accepted His Grace's amendment with pleasure. He considered it the brightest amendment His Grace had made that week. The Government, he said, was aware of the intimate relation in which His Grace stood to the bottom end of a parallelogram and was prepared to respect it.

Lord Halifax rose to offer a further amendment. He thought the present case was one in which the "four-fifths" clause ought to apply: he should wish it stated that the angles are equal for two days every week, except in the case of schools where four-fifths of the parents are conscientiously opposed to the use of the isosceles triangle.

The Leader of the Government thought the amendment was a singularly pleasing one. He accepted it and would like it understood that the words isosceles triangle were not meant in any offensive sense.

Lord Rosebery spoke at some length. He considered the clause unfair to Scotland where the high state of morality rendered education unnecessary. Unless an amendment in this sense was accepted, it might be necessary to reconsider the Act of Union of 1707.

The Leader of the Government said that Lord Rosebery's amendment was the best he had heard yet. The Government accepted it at once. They were willing to make every concession. They would, if need be, reconsider the Norman Conquest.

The Duke of Devonshire took exception to the part of the clause relating to the production of the sides. He did not think the country was prepared for it. It was unfair to the producer. He would like the clause altered to read, "if the sides be produced in the home market."

The Leader of the Government accepted with pleasure His Grace's amendment. He considered it quite sensible. He would now, as it was near the hour of rising, present the clause in its revised form. He hoped, however, that their Lordships would find time to think out some further amendments for the evening sitting.

The clause was then read.

His Grace of Canterbury then moved that the House, in all humility, adjourn for dinner.

THE CONJURER'S REVENGE

"Now, ladies and gentlemen," said the conjurer, "having shown you that the cloth is absolutely empty, I will proceed to take from it a bowl of goldfish. Presto!"

All around the hall people were saying, "Oh, how wonderful! How does he do it?"

But the Quick Man on the front seat said in a big

whisper to the people near him, "He—had—it—up—his—sleeve."

Then the people nodded brightly at the Quick Man and said, "Oh, of course"; and everybody whispered round the hall, "He—had—it—up—his—sleeve."

"My next trick," said the conjurer, "is the famous Hindostanee rings. You will notice that the rings are apparently separate; at a blow they all join (clang, clang, clang)—Presto!"

There was a general buzz of stupefaction till the Quick Man was heard to whisper, "He—must—have—had—another—lot—up—his—sleeve."

Again everybody nodded and whispered, "The—rings—were—up—his—sleeve."

The brow of the conjurer was clouded with a gathering frown.

"I will now," he continued, "show you a most amusing trick by which I am enabled to take any number of eggs from a hat. Will some gentleman kindly lend me his hat? Ah, thank you—Presto!"

He extracted seventeen eggs, and for thirty-five seconds the audience began to think that he was wonderful. Then the Quick Man whispered along the front bench, "He—has—a—hen—up—his—sleeve," and all the people whispered it on. "He—has—a—lot—of—hens—up—his—sleeve."

The egg trick was ruined.

It went on like that all through. It transpired from the whispers of the Quick Man that the conjurer must have concealed up his sleeve, in addition to the rings, hens, and fish, several packs of cards, a loaf of bread, a doll's cradle, a live guinea-pig, a fifty-cent piece, and a rocking-chair.

The reputation of the conjurer was rapidly sinking

below zero. At the close of the evening he rallied for a final effort.

"Ladies and gentlemen," he said, "I will present to you, in conclusion, the famous Japanese trick recently invented by the natives of Tipperary. Will you, sir," he continued, turning toward the Quick Man, "will you kindly hand me your gold watch?"

It was passed to him.

"Have I your permission to put it into this mortar and pound it to pieces?" he asked savagely.

The Quick Man nodded and smiled.

The conjurer threw the watch into the mortar and grasped a sledge hammer from the table. There was a sound of violent smashing. "He's—slipped—it—up—his—sleeve," whispered the Quick Man.

"Now, sir," continued the conjurer, "will you allow me to take your handkerchief and punch holes in it? Thank you. You see, ladies and gentlemen, there is no deception, the holes are visible to the eye."

The face of the Quick Man beamed. This time the real mystery of the thing fascinated him.

"And now, sir, will you kindly pass me your silk hat and allow me to dance on it? Thank you."

The conjurer made a few rapid passes with his feet and exhibited the hat crushed beyond recognition.

"And will you now, sir, take off your celluloid collar and permit me to burn it in the candle? Thank you, sir. And will you allow me to smash your spectacles for you with my hammer? Thank you."

By this time the features of the Quick Man were assuming a puzzled expression. "This thing beats me," he whispered, "I don't see through it a bit."

There was a great hush upon the audience. Then the

conjurer drew himself up to his full height and, with a withering look at the Quick Man, he concluded:

"Ladies and gentlemen, you will observe that I have, with this gentleman's permission, broken his watch, burnt his collar, smashed his spectacles, and danced on his hat. If he will give me the further permission to paint green stripes on his overcoat, or to tie his suspenders in a knot, I shall be delighted to entertain you. If not, the performance is at an end."

And amid a glorious burst of music from the orchestra the curtain fell, and the audience dispersed, convinced that there are some tricks, at any rate, that are not done up the conjurer's sleeve.

HINTS TO TRAVELLERS

THE following hints and observations have occurred to me during a recent trip across the continent: they are written in no spirit of complaint against existing railroad methods, but merely in the hope that they may prove useful to those who travel, like myself, in a spirit of meek, observant ignorance.

1. Sleeping in a Pullman car presents some difficulties to the novice. Care should be taken to allay all sense of danger. The frequent whistling of the engine during the night is apt to be a source of alarm. Find out, therefore, before travelling, the meaning of the various whistles. One means "station," two, "rail-road crossing," and so on. Five whistles, short and rapid, mean sudden danger. When you hear whistles in the night, sit up smartly in your bunk and count them. Should they reach five, draw

on your trousers over your pyjamas and leave the train instantly. As a further precaution against accident, sleep with the feet towards the engine if you prefer to have the feet crushed, or with the head towards the engine, if you think it best to have the head crushed. In making this decision try to be as unselfish as possible. If indifferent, sleep crosswise with the head hanging over into the aisle.

2. I have devoted some thought to the proper method of changing trains. The system which I have observed to be the most popular with travellers of my own class, is something as follows: Suppose that you have been told on leaving New York that you are to change at Kansas City. The evening before approaching Kansas City, stop the conductor in the aisle of the car (you can do this best by putting out your foot and tripping him), and say politely, "Do I change at Kansas City?" He says "Yes." Very good. Don't believe him. On going into the dining-car for supper, take a negro aside and put it to him as a personal matter between a white man and a black, whether he thinks you ought to change at Kansas City. Don't be satisfied with this. In the course of the evening pass through the entire train from time to time, and say to people casually, "Oh, can you tell me if I change at Kansas City?" Ask the conductor about it a few more times in the evening: a repetition of the question will ensure pleasant relations with him. Before falling asleep watch for his passage and ask him through the curtains of your berth, "Oh, by the way, did you say I changed at Kansas City?" If he refuses to stop, hook him by the neck with your walking-stick, and draw him gently to your bedside. In the morning when the train stops and a man calls, "Kansas City! All change!" approach the conductor and say, "Is this Kansas City?"

Don't be discouraged at his answer. Pick yourself up and go to the other end of the car and say to the brakesman, "Do you know, sir, if this is Kansas City?" Don't be too easily convinced. Remember that both brakesman and conductor may be in collusion to deceive you. Look around, therefore, for the name of the station on the signboard. Having found it, alight and ask the first man you see if this is Kansas City. He will answer, "Why, where in blank are your blank eyes? Can't you see it there, plain as blank?" When you hear language of this sort, ask no more. You are now in Kansas and this is Kansas City.

3. I have observed that it is now the practice of the conductors to stick bits of paper in the hats of the passengers. They do this, I believe, to mark which ones they like best. The device is pretty, and adds much to the scenic appearance of the car. But I notice with pain that the system is fraught with much trouble for the conductors. The task of crushing two or three passengers together, in order to reach over them and stick a ticket into the chinks of a silk skull cap is embarrassing for a conductor of refined feelings. It would be simpler if the conductor should carry a small hammer and a packet of shingle nails and nail the paid-up passenger to the back of the seat. Or better still, let the conductor carry a small pot of paint and a brush, and mark the passengers in such a way that he cannot easily mistake them. In the case of bald-headed passengers, the hats might be politely removed and red crosses painted on the craniums. This will indicate that they are bald. Through passengers might be distinguished by a complete coat of paint. In the hands of a man of taste, much might be effected by a little grouping of painted passengers and the leisure time of the conductor agreeably occupied.

4. I have observed in travelling in the West that the irregularity of railroad accidents is a fruitful cause of complaint. The frequent disappointment of the holders of accident-policy tickets on western roads is leading to widespread protest. Certainly the conditions of travel in the West are altering rapidly and accidents can no longer be relied upon. This is deeply to be regretted, in so much as, apart from accidents, the tickets may be said to be practically valueless.

A MANUAL OF EDUCATION

THE few selections below are offered as a specimen page of a little book which I have in course of preparation.

Every man has somewhere in the back of his head the wreck of a thing which he calls his education. My book is intended to embody in concise form these remnants of early instruction.

Educations are divided into splendid educations, thorough classical educations, and average educations. All very old men have splendid educations; all men who apparently know nothing else have thorough classical educations; nobody has an average education.

An education, when it is all written out on foolscap, covers nearly ten sheets. It takes about six years of severe college training to acquire it. Even then a man often finds that he somehow hasn't got his education just where he can put his thumb on it. When my little book of eight or ten pages has appeared, everybody may carry his education in his hip pocket.

Those who have not had the advantage of an early training will be enabled, by a few hours of conscientious application, to put themselves on an equal footing with the most scholarly.

The selections are chosen entirely at random.

I.—REMAINS OF ASTRONOMY

Astronomy teaches the correct use of the sun and the planets. These may be put on a frame of little sticks and turned round. This causes the tides. Those at the ends of the sticks are enormously far away. From time to time a diligent search of the sticks reveals new planets. The orbit of a planet is the distance the stick goes round in going round. Astronomy is intensely interesting; it should be done at night, in a high tower in Spitzbergen. This is to avoid the astronomy being interrupted. A really good astronomer can tell when a comet is coming too near him by the warning buzz of the revolving sticks.

II.—REMAINS OF HISTORY

Aztecs: A fabulous race, half man, half horse, half mound-builder. They flourished at about the same time as the early Calithumpians. They have left some awfully stupendous monuments of themselves somewhere.

Life of Cæsar: A famous Roman general, the last who ever landed in Britain without being stopped at the custom house. On returning to his Sabine farm (to fetch something), he was stabbed by Brutus, and died with the words "Veni, vidi, tekel, upharsim" in his throat. The jury returned a verdict of strangulation.

Life of Voltaire: A Frenchman; very bitter.

Life of Schopenhauer: A German; very deep; but it was not really noticeable when he sat down.

Life of Dante: An Italian; the first to introduce the

banana and the class of street organ known as "Dante's Inferno."

Peter the Great, Alfred the Great, Frederick the Great, John the Great, Tom the Great, Jim the Great, Jo the Great, etc., etc.	It is impossible for a busy man to keep these apart. They sought a living as kings and apostles and pugilists and so on.

III.—REMAINS OF BOTANY

Botany is the art of plants. Plants are divided into trees, flowers, and vegetables. The true botanist knows a tree as soon as he sees it. He learns to distinguish it from a vegetable by merely putting his ear to it.

IV.—REMAINS OF NATURAL SCIENCE

Natural Science treats of motion and force. Many of its teachings remain as part of an educated man's permanent equipment in life.

Such are:

(*a*) The harder you shove a bicycle the faster it will go. This is because of natural science.

(*b*) If you fall from a high tower, you fall quicker and quicker and quicker; a judicious selection of a tower will ensure any rate of speed.

(*c*) If you put your thumb in between two cogs it will go on and on, until the wheels are arrested, by your suspenders. This is machinery.

(*d*) Electricity is of two kinds, positive and negative. The difference is, I presume, that one kind comes a little more expensive, but is more durable; the other is a cheaper thing, but the moths get into it.

HOODOO McFIGGIN'S CHRISTMAS

THIS Santa Claus business is played out. It's a sneaking, underhand method, and the sooner it's exposed the better.

For a parent to get up under cover of the darkness of night and palm off a ten-cent necktie on a boy who had been expecting a ten-dollar watch, and then say that an angel sent it to him, is low, undeniably low.

I had a good opportunity of observing how the thing worked this Christmas, in the case of young Hoodoo McFiggin, the son and heir of the McFiggins, at whose house I board.

Hoodoo McFiggin is a good boy—a religious boy. He had been given to understand that Santa Claus would bring nothing to his father and mother because grown-up people don't get presents from the angels. So he saved up all his pocket-money and bought a box of cigars for his father and a seventy-five-cent diamond brooch for his mother. His own fortunes he left in the hands of the angels. But he prayed. He prayed every night for weeks that Santa Claus would bring him a pair of skates and a puppy-dog and an air-gun and a bicycle and a Noah's ark and a sleigh and a drum—altogether about a hundred and fifty dollars' worth of stuff.

I went into Hoodoo's room quite early Christmas morning. I had an idea that the scene would be interesting. I woke him up and he sat up in bed, his eyes glistening with radiant expectation, and began hauling things out of his stocking.

The first parcel was bulky; it was done up quite loosely and had an odd look generally.

"Ha! ha!" Hoodoo cried gleefully, as he began undoing it. "I'll bet it's the puppy-dog, all wrapped up in paper!"

And was it the puppy-dog? No, by no means. It was a pair of nice, strong, number-four boots, laces and all, labelled, "Hoodoo, from Santa Claus," and underneath Santa Claus had written, "95 net."

The boy's jaw fell with delight. "It's boots," he said, and plunged in his hand again.

He began hauling away at another parcel with renewed hope on his face.

This time the thing seemed like a little round box. Hoodoo tore the paper off it with a feverish hand. He shook it; something rattled inside.

"It's a watch and chain! It's a watch and chain!" he shouted. Then he pulled the lid off.

And was it a watch and chain? No. It was a box of nice, brand-new celluloid collars, a dozen of them all alike and all his own size.

The boy was so pleased that you could see his face crack up with pleasure.

He waited a few minutes until his intense joy subsided. Then he tried again.

This time the packet was long and hard. It resisted the touch and had a sort of funnel shape.

"It's a toy pistol!" said the boy, trembling with excitement. "Gee! I hope there are lots of caps with it! I'll fire some off now and wake up father."

No, my poor child, you will not wake your father with that. It is a useful thing, but it needs not caps and it fires no bullets, and you cannot wake a sleeping man with a tooth-brush. Yes, it was a tooth-brush—a regular beauty, pure bone all through, and ticketed with a little paper, "Hoodoo, from Santa Claus."

Again the expression of intense joy passed over the boy's face, and the tears of gratitude started from his eyes. He wiped them away with his tooth-brush and passed on.

The next packet was much larger and evidently contained something soft and bulky. It had been too long to go into the stocking and was tied outside.

"I wonder what this is," Hoodoo mused, half afraid to open it. Then his heart gave a great leap, and he forgot all his other presents in the anticipation of this one. "It's the drum, all wrapped up!"

Drum nothing! It was pants—a pair of the nicest little short pants—yellowish-brown short pants—with dear little stripes of colour running across both ways, and here again Santa Claus had written, "Hoodoo, from Santa Claus, one fort net."

But there was something wrapped up in it. Oh, yes! There was a pair of braces wrapped up in it, braces with a little steel sliding thing so that you could slide your pants up to your neck, if you wanted to.

The boy gave a dry sob of satisfaction. Then he took out his last present. "It's a book," he said, as he unwrapped it. "I wonder if it is fairy stories or adventures. Oh, I hope it's adventures! I'll read it all morning."

No, Hoodoo, it was not precisely adventures. It was a small family Bible. Hoodoo had now seen all his presents, and he arose and dressed. But he still had the fun of playing with his toys. That is always the chief delight of Christmas morning.

First he played with his tooth-brush. He got a whole lot of water and brushed all his teeth with it. This was huge.

Then he played with his collars. He had no end of fun with them, taking them all out one by one and swearing at them, and then putting them back and swearing at the whole lot together.

The next toy was his pants. He had immense fun there, putting them on and taking them off again, and then trying to guess which side was which by merely looking at them.

After that he took his book and read some adventures called "Genesis" till breakfast-time.

Then he went downstairs and kissed his father and mother. His father was smoking a cigar, and his mother had her new brooch on. Hoodoo's face was thoughtful, and a light seemed to have broken in upon his mind. Indeed, I think it altogether likely that next Christmas he will hang on to his own money and take chances on what the angels bring.

THE LIFE OF JOHN SMITH

THE lives of great men occupy a large section of our literature. The great man is certainly a wonderful thing. He walks across his century and leaves the marks of his feet all over it, ripping out the dates on his goloshes as he passes. It is impossible to get up a revolution or a new religion, or a national awakening of any sort, without his turning up, putting himself at the head of it and collaring all the gate-receipts for himself. Even after his death he leaves a long trail of second-rate relations spattered over the front seats of fifty years of history.

Now the lives of great men are doubtless infinitely

interesting. But at times I must confess to a sense of reaction and an idea that the ordinary common man is entitled to have his biography written too. It is to illustrate this view that I write the life of John Smith, a man neither good nor great, but just the usual, everyday homo like you and me and the rest of us.

From his earliest childhood John Smith was marked out from his comrades by nothing. The marvellous precocity of the boy did not astonish his preceptors. Books were not a passion for him from his youth, neither did any old man put his hand on Smith's head and say, mark his words, this boy would some day become a man. Nor yet was it his father's wont to gaze on him with a feeling amounting almost to awe. By no means! All his father did was to wonder whether Smith was a darn fool because he couldn't help it, or because he thought it smart. In other words, he was just like you and me and the rest of us.

In those athletic sports which were the ornament of the youth of his day, Smith did not, as great men do, excel his fellows. He couldn't ride worth a darn. He couldn't skate worth a darn. He couldn't swim worth a darn. He couldn't shoot worth a darn. He couldn't do anything worth a darn. He was just like us.

Nor did the bold cast of the boy's mind offset his physical defects, as it invariably does in the biographies. On the contrary. He was afraid of his father. He was afraid of his school-teacher. He was afraid of dogs. He was afraid of guns. He was afraid of lightning. He was afraid of hell. He was afraid of girls.

In the boy's choice of a profession there was not seen that keen longing for a life-work that we find in the celebrities. He didn't want to be a lawyer, because you have to know law. He didn't want to be a doctor, because you have to know medicine. He didn't want to be a business-man, because you have to know business; and he didn't want to be a school-teacher, because he had seen too many of them. As far as he had any choice, it lay between being Robinson Crusoe and being the Prince of Wales. His father refused him both and put him into a dry-goods establishment.

Such was the childhood of Smith. At its close there was nothing in his outward appearance to mark the man of genius. The casual observer could have seen no genius concealed behind the wide face, the massive mouth, the long slanting forehead, and the tall ear that swept up to the close-cropped head. Certainly he couldn't. There wasn't any concealed there.

It was shortly after his start in business life that Smith was stricken with the first of those distressing attacks, to which he afterwards became subject. It seized him late one night as he was returning home from a delightful evening of song and praise with a few old school chums. Its symptoms were a peculiar heaving of the sidewalk, a dancing of the street lights, and a crafty shifting to and fro of the houses, requiring a very nice discrimination in selecting his own. There was a strong desire not to drink water throughout the entire attack, which showed that the thing was evidently a form of hydrophobia. From this time on, these painful attacks became chronic with Smith. They were liable to come on at any time, but especially on Saturday nights, on the first of the month, and on Thanksgiving Day. He always had a very severe attack of hydrophobia on Christmas Eve, and after elections it was fearful.

There was one incident in Smith's career which he did, perhaps, share with regret. He had scarcely reached manhood when he met the most beautiful girl in the world. She was different from all other women. She had a deeper nature than other people. Smith realised it at once. She could feel and understand things that ordinary people couldn't. She could understand him. She had a great sense of humour and an exquisite appreciation of a joke. He told her the six that he knew one night and she thought them great. Her mere presence made Smith feel as if he had swallowed a sunset: the first time that his finger brushed against hers, he felt a thrill all through him. He presently found that if he took a firm hold of her hand with his, he could get a fine thrill, and if he sat beside her on a sofa, with his head against her ear and his arm about once and a half round her, he could get what you might call a first-class, A-1 thrill. Smith became filled with the idea that he would like to have her always near him. He suggested an arrangement to her, by which she should come and live in the same house with him and take personal charge of his clothes and his meals. She was to receive in return her board and washing, about seventy-five cents a week in ready money, and Smith was to be her slave.

After Smith had been this woman's slave for some time, baby fingers stole across his life, then another set of them, and then more and more till the house was full of them. The woman's mother began to steal across his life, too, and every time she came Smith had hydrophobia frightfully. Strangely enough there was no little prattler that was taken from his life and became a saddened, hallowed memory to him. Oh, no! The little Smiths were not that kind of prattler. The whole nine grew up into tall, lank boys with massive mouths and great sweeping ears like their father's, and no talent for anything.

The life of Smith never seemed to bring him to any of

those great turning-points that occurred in the lives of the great. True, the passing years brought some change of fortune. He was moved up in his dry-goods establishment from the ribbon counter to the collar counter, from the collar counter to the gents' panting counter, and from the gents' panting to the gents' fancy shirting. Then, as he grew aged and inefficient, they moved him down again from the gents' fancy shirting to the gents' panting, and so on to the ribbon counter. And when he grew quite old they dismissed him and got a boy with a four-inch mouth and sandy-coloured hair, who did all Smith could do for half the money. That was John Smith's mercantile career: it won't stand comparison with Mr. Gladstone's, but it's not unlike your own.

Smith lived for five years after this. His sons kept him. They didn't want to, but they had to. In his old age the brightness of his mind and his fund of anecdote were *not* the delight of all who dropped in to see him. He told seven stories and he knew six jokes. The stories were long things all about himself, and the jokes were about a commercial traveller and a Methodist minister. But nobody dropped in to see him, anyway, so it didn't matter.

At sixty-five Smith was taken ill, and, receiving proper treatment, he died. There was a tombstone put up over him, with a hand pointing north-north-east.

But I doubt if he ever got there. He was too like us.

ON COLLECTING THINGS

LIKE most other men, I have from time to time been stricken with a desire to make collections of things.

It began with postage stamps. I had a letter from a friend of mine who had gone out to South Africa. The letter had a three-cornered stamp on it, and I thought as soon as I looked at it, "That's the thing! Stamp collecting! I'll devote my life to it."

I bought an album with accommodation for the stamps of all nations, and began collecting right off. For three days the collection made wonderful progress. It contained:

One Cape of Good Hope stamp.

One one-cent stamp, United States of America.

One two-cent stamp, United States of America.

One five-cent stamp, United States of America.

One ten-cent stamp, United States of America.

After that the collection came to a dead stop. For a while I used to talk about it rather airily and say I had one or two rather valuable South African stamps. But I presently grew tired even of lying about it.

Collecting coins is a thing that I attempt at intervals. Every time I am given an old half-penny or a Mexican quarter, I get an idea that if a fellow made a point of holding on to rarities of that sort, he'd soon have quite a valuable collection. The first time that I tried it I was full of enthusiasm, and before long my collection numbered quite a few articles of vertu. The items were as follows:

No. 1. Ancient Roman coin. Time of Caligula. This one of course was the gem of the whole lot; it was given me by a friend, and that was what started me collecting.

No. 2. Small copper coin. Value one cent. United States of America. Apparently modern.

No. 3. Small nickel coin. Circular. United States of America. Value five cents.

No. 4. Small silver coin. Value ten cents. United States of America.

No. 5. Silver coin. Circular. Value twenty-five cents. United States of America. Very beautiful.

No. 6. Large silver coin. Circular. Inscription, "One Dollar." United States of America. Very valuable.

No. 7. Ancient British copper coin. Probably time of Caractacus. Very dim. Inscription, "Victoria Dei gratia regina." Very valuable.

No. 8. Silver coin. Evidently French. Inscription, "Fünf Mark. Kaiser Wilhelm."

No. 9. Circular silver coin. Very much defaced. Part of inscription, "E Pluribus Unum." Probably a Russian rouble, but quite as likely to be a Japanese yen or a Shanghai rooster.

That's as far as that collection got. It lasted through most of the winter and I was getting quite proud of it, but I took the coins down town one evening to show to a friend and we spent No. 3, No. 4, No. 5, No. 6 and No. 7 in buying a little dinner for two. After dinner I bought a yen's worth of cigars and traded the relic of Caligula for as many hot Scotches as they cared to advance on it. After that I felt reckless and put No. 2 and No. 8 into a Children's Hospital poor box.

I tried fossils next. I got two in ten years. Then I quit.

A friend of mine once showed me a very fine collection of ancient and curious weapons, and for a time I was full of that idea. I gathered several interesting specimens, such as:

No. 1. Old flint-lock musket, used by my grandfather. (He used it on the farm for years as a crowbar.)

No. 2. Old raw-hide strap, used by my father.

No. 3. Ancient Indian arrowhead, found by myself the very day after I began collecting. It resembles a three-cornered stone.

No. 4. Ancient Indian bow, found by myself behind a sawmill on the second day of my collecting. It resembles a straight stick of elm or oak. It is interesting to think that this very weapon may have figured in some fierce scene of savage warfare.

No. 5. Cannibal poniard or straight-handled dagger of the South Sea Islands. It will give the reader almost a thrill of horror to learn that this atrocious weapon, which I bought myself on the third day of collecting, was actually exposed in a second-hand store as a family carving-knife. In gazing at it one cannot refrain from conjuring up the awful scenes it must have witnessed.

I kept this collection for quite a long while until, in a moment of infatuation, I presented it to a young lady as a betrothal present. The gift proved too ostentatious and our relations subsequently ceased to be cordial.

On the whole I am inclined to recommend the beginner to confine himself to collecting coins. At present I am myself making a collection of American bills (time of Taft preferred), a pursuit I find most absorbing.

SOCIETY CHIT-CHAT

AS IT SHOULD BE WRITTEN

I NOTICE that it is customary for the daily papers to publish a column or so of society gossip. They generally head it "Chit-Chat," or "On Dit," or "Le Boudoir," or something of the sort, and they keep it pretty full of French terms to give it the proper sort of swing. These columns may be very interesting in their way, but it always seems to me that they don't get hold of quite the right things to tell us about. They are very fond, for instance, of giving an account of the delightful dance at Mrs. De Smythe's—at which Mrs. De Smythe looked charming in a gown of old tulle with a stomacher of passementerie—or of the dinner-party at Mr. Alonzo Robinson's residence, or the smart pink tea given by Miss Carlotta Jones. No, that's all right, but it's not the kind of thing we want to get at; those are not the events which happen in our neighbours' houses that we really want to hear about. It is the quiet little family scenes, the little traits of home-life that—well, for example, take the case of that delightful party at the De Smythes. I am certain that all those who were present would much prefer a little paragraph like the following, which would give them some idea of the home-life of the De Smythes on the morning after the party.

DEJEUNER DE LUXE AT THE DE SMYTHE RESIDENCE

On Wednesday morning last at 7.15 a.m. a charming little breakfast was served at the home of Mr. De Smythe.

The *déjeuner* was given in honour of Mr. De Smythe and his two sons, Master Adolphus and Master Blinks De Smythe, who were about to leave for their daily *travail* at their wholesale *Bureau de Flour et de Feed*. All the gentlemen were very quietly dressed in their *habits de work*. Miss Melinda De Smythe poured out tea, the *domestique* having *refusé* to get up so early after the *partie* of the night before. The menu was very handsome, consisting of eggs and bacon, *demi-froid*, and ice-cream. The conversation was sustained and lively. Mr. De Smythe sustained it and made it lively for his daughter and his *garçons*. In the course of the talk Mr. De Smythe stated that the next time he allowed the young people to turn his *maison* topsy-turvy he would see them in *enfer*. He wished to know if they were aware that some ass of the evening before had broken a pane of coloured glass in the hall that would cost him four dollars. Did they think he was made of *argent*. If so, they never made a bigger mistake in their *vie*. The meal closed with general expressions of good-feeling. A little bird has whispered to us that there will be no more parties at the De Smythes' *pour long-temps*.

Here is another little paragraph that would be of general interest in society.

DINER DE FAMEEL AT THE BOARDING-HOUSE DE MCFIGGIN

Yesterday evening at half after six a pleasant little *diner* was given by Madame McFiggin of Rock Street, to her boarders. The *salle à manger* was very prettily decorated with texts, and the furniture upholstered with *cheveux de horse, Louis Quinze*. The boarders were all very quietly dressed: Mrs. McFiggin was daintily attired in some old clinging stuff with a *corsage de*

Whalebone underneath. The ample board groaned under the bill of fare. The boarders groaned also. Their groaning was very noticeable. The *pièce de résistance* was a *hunko de bœuf boilé*, flanked with some old clinging stuff. The *entrées* were *pâté de pumpkin*, followed by *fromage McFiggin*, served under glass. Towards the end of the first course, speeches became the order of the day. Mrs. McFiggin was the first speaker. In commencing, she expressed her surprise that so few of the gentlemen seemed to care for the *hunko de bœuf;* her own mind, she said, had hesitated between *hunko de bœuf boilé* and a pair of roast chickens (sensation). She had finally decided in favour of the *hunko de bœuf* (no sensation). She referred at some length to the late Mr. McFiggin, who had always shown a marked preference for *hunko de bœuf*. Several other speakers followed. All spoke forcibly and to the point. The last to speak was the Reverend Mr. Whiner. The reverend gentleman, in rising, said that he confided himself and his fellow-boarders to the special interference of Providence. For what they had eaten, he said, he hoped that Providence would make them truly thankful. At the close of the *Repas* several of the boarders expressed their *intention* of going down the street to a *restourong* to get *quelque chose à manger*.

Here is another example. How interesting it would be to get a detailed account of that little affair at the Robinsons', of which the neighbours only heard indirectly! Thus:

DELIGHTFUL EVENING AT THE RESIDENCE OF MR. ALONZO ROBINSON

Yesterday the family of Mr. Alonzo Robinson spent a very lively evening at their home on ——th Avenue.

The occasion was the seventeenth birthday of Master Alonzo Robinson, junior. It was the original intention of Master Alonzo Robinson to celebrate the day at home and invite a few of *les garçons*. Mr. Robinson, senior, however, having declared that he would be *damné* first, Master Alonzo spent the evening in visiting the *salons* of the town, which he painted *rouge*. Mr. Robinson, senior, spent the evening at home in quiet expectation of his son's return. He was very becomingly dressed in a *pantalon quatre vingt treize*, and had his *whippe de chien* laid across his knee. Madame Robinson and the Mademoiselles Robinson wore black. The guest of the evening arrived at a late hour. He wore his *habits de spri*, and had about six *pouces* of *eau de vie* in him. He was evidently full up to his *cou*. For some time after his arrival a very lively time was spent. Mr. Robinson having at length broken the *whippe de chien*, the family parted for the night with expressions of cordial goodwill.

INSURANCE UP TO DATE

A MAN called on me the other day with the idea of insuring my life. Now, I detest life-insurance agents; they always argue that I shall some day die, which is not so. I have been insured a great many times, for about a month at a time, but have had no luck with it at all.

So I made up my mind that I would outwit this man at his own game. I let him talk straight ahead and encouraged him all I could, until he finally left me with a sheet of questions which I was to answer as an applicant. Now this was what I was waiting for; I had decided that, if the company wanted information about me, they should have it, and have the very best quality I could supply. So I spread the sheet of questions before me, and drew up a set of answers for them, which, I hoped, would settle for ever all doubts to my eligibility for insurance.

Question.—What is your age?

Answer.—I can't think.

Q.—What is your chest measurement?

A.—Nineteen inches.

Q.—What is your chest expansion?

A.—Half an inch.

Q.—What is your height?

A.—Six feet five, if erect, but less when I walk on all fours.

Q.—Is your grandfather dead?

A.—Practically.

Q.—Cause of death, if dead?

A.—Dipsomania, if dead.

Q.—Is your father dead?

A.—To the world.

Q.—Cause of death?

A.—Hydrophobia.

Q.—Place of father's residence?

A.—Kentucky.

Q.—What illnesses have you had?

A.—As a child, consumption, leprosy, and water on the knee. As a man, whooping-cough, stomach-ache, and water on the brain.

Q.—Have you any brothers?

A.—Thirteen; all nearly dead.

Q.—Are you aware of any habits or tendencies which might be expected to shorten your life?

A.—I am aware. I drink, I smoke, I take morphine and vaseline. I swallow grape seeds and I hate exercise.

I thought when I had come to the end of that list that I had made a dead sure thing of it, and I posted the paper with a cheque for three months' payment, feeling pretty confident of having the cheque sent back to me. I was a good deal surprised a few days later to receive the following letter from the company:

"DEAR SIR,—We beg to acknowledge your letter of application and cheque for fifteen dollars. After a careful comparison of your case with the average modern standard, we are pleased to accept you as a first-class risk."

BORROWING A MATCH

YOU might think that borrowing a match upon the street is a simple thing. But any man who has ever tried it will assure you that it is not, and will be prepared to swear on oath to the truth of my experience of the other evening.

I was standing on the corner of the street with a cigar that I wanted to light. I had no match. I waited till a decent, ordinary man came along. Then I said:

"Excuse me, sir, but could you oblige me with the loan of a match?"

"A match?" he said, "why, certainly." Then he unbuttoned his overcoat and put his hand in the pocket of his waistcoat. "I know I have one," he went on, "and I'd almost swear it's in the bottom pocket—or, hold on, though, I guess it may be in the top—just wait till I put these parcels down on the sidewalk."

"Oh, don't trouble," I said, "It's really of no consequence."

"Oh, it's no trouble, I'll have it in a minute; I know there must be one in here somewhere"—he was digging his fingers into his pockets as he spoke—"but you see this isn't the waistcoat I generally . . ."

I saw that the man was getting excited about it. "Well, never mind," I protested; "if that isn't the waistcoat that you generally—why, it doesn't matter."

"Hold on, now, hold on!" the man said, "I've got one of the cursed things in here somewhere. I guess it must be in with my watch. No, it's not there either. Wait till I try my coat. If that confounded tailor only knew enough to make a pocket so that a man could get at it!"

He was getting pretty well worked up now. He had thrown down his walking-stick and was plunging at his pockets with his teeth set. "It's that cursed young boy of mine," he hissed; "this comes of his fooling in my pockets. By Gad! perhaps I won't warm him up when I get home. Say, I'll bet that it's in my hip-pocket. You just hold up the tail of my overcoat a second till I . . ."

"No, no," I protested again, "please don't take all this trouble, it really doesn't matter. I'm sure you needn't take off your overcoat, and oh, pray don't throw away your letters and things in the snow like that, and tear out your pockets by the roots! Please, please don't trample over your overcoat and put your feet through the parcels. I do hate to hear you swearing at your little boy, with that peculiar whine in your voice. Don't—please don't tear your clothes so savagely."

Suddenly the man gave a grunt of exultation, and drew his hand up from inside the lining of his coat.

"I've got it," he cried. "Here you are!" Then he brought it out under the light.

It was a toothpick.

Yielding to the impulse of the moment I pushed him under the wheels of a trolley-car and ran.

A LESSON IN FICTION

SUPPOSE that in the opening pages of the modern melodramatic novel you find some such situation as the following, in which is depicted the terrific combat between Gaspard de Vaux, the boy lieutenant, and Hairy Hank, the chief of the Italian banditti:

"The inequality of the contest was apparent. With a mingled yell of rage and contempt, his sword brandished above his head and his dirk between his teeth, the enormous bandit rushed upon his intrepid opponent. De Vaux seemed scarce more than a stripling, but he stood his ground and faced his hitherto invincible assailant. 'Mong Dieu,' cried De Smythe, 'he is lost!' "

Question.—On which of the parties to the above contest do you honestly feel inclined to put your money?

Answer.—On De Vaux. He'll win. Hairy Hank will force him down to one knee and with a brutal cry of "Har! har!" will be about to dirk him, when De Vaux will make a sudden lunge (one he had learnt at home out of a book of lunges) and——

Very good. You have answered correctly. Now, suppose you find, a little later in the book, that the killing of Hairy Hank has compelled De Vaux to flee from his native land to the East. Are you not fearful for his safety in the desert?

Answer.—Frankly, I am not. De Vaux is all right. His name is on the title page, and you can't kill him.

Question.—Listen to this, then: "The sun of Ethiopia beat fiercely upon the desert as De Vaux, mounted upon his faithful elephant, pursued his lonely way. Seated in his lofty hoo-doo, his eye scoured the waste. Suddenly a solitary horseman appeared on the horizon, then another, and another, and then six. In a few moments a whole crowd of solitary horsemen swooped down upon him. There was a fierce shout of 'Allah!' a rattle of fire-arms. De Vaux sank from his hoo-doo on to the sands, while the affrighted elephant dashed off in all directions. The bullet had struck him in the heart."

There now, what do you think of that? Isn't De Vaux killed now?

Answer.—I am sorry. De Vaux is not dead. True, the ball had hit him, oh yes, it had hit him, but it had glanced off against a family Bible, which he carried in his waist-coat in case of illness, struck some hymns that he had in his hip-pocket, and, glancing off again, had flattened itself against De Vaux's diary of his life in the desert, which was in his knapsack.

Question.—But even if this doesn't kill him, you must admit that he is near death when he is bitten in the jungle by the deadly dongola?

Answer.—That's all right. A kindly Arab will take De Vaux to the Sheik's tent.

Question.—What will De Vaux remind the Sheik of?

Answer.—Too easy. Of his long-lost son who disappeared years ago.

Question.—Was this son Hairy Hank?

Answer.—Of course he was. Anyone could see that but the Sheik never suspects it, and heals De Vaux. He heals him with an herb, a thing called a simple, an amazingly simple, known only to the Sheik. Since using this herb, the Sheik has used no other.

Question.—The Sheik will recognise an overcoat that De Vaux is wearing, and complications will arise in the matter of Hairy Hank deceased. Will this result in the death of the boy lieutenant?

Answer.—No. By this time De Vaux has realised that the reader knows he won't die, and resolves to quit the desert. The thought of his mother keeps recurring to him, and of his father, too, the grey, stooping old man—does he stoop still or has he stopped stooping? At times, too, there comes the thought of another, a fairer than his father; she whose—but enough, De Vaux returns to the old homestead in Piccadilly.

Question.—When De Vaux returns to England, what will happen?

Answer.—This will happen: "He who left England ten years before a raw boy, has returned a sunburnt soldierly man. But who is this that advances smilingly to meet him? Can the mere girl, the bright child that shared his hours of play, can she have grown into this peerless, graceful girl, at whose feet half the noble suitors of England are kneeling? 'Can this be her?' he asks himself in amazement."

Question.—Is it her?

Answer.—Oh, it's her all right. It is her, and it is him, and it is them. That girl hasn't waited fifty pages for nothing.

Question.—You evidently guess that a love affair will ensue between the boy lieutenant and the peerless girl with the broad feet. Do you imagine, however, that its course will run smoothly and leave nothing to record?

Answer.—Not at all. I feel certain that the scene of the novel having edged itself around to London, the writer will not feel satisfied unless he introduces the following famous scene:

"Stunned by the cruel revelation which he had received, unconscious of whither his steps were taking him, Gaspard de Vaux wandered on in the darkness from street to street until he found himself upon London Bridge. He leaned over the parapet and looked down upon the whirling stream below. There was something in the still, swift rush of it that seemed to beckon, to allure him. After all, why not? What was life now that he should prize it? For a moment De Vaux paused irresolute."

Question.—Will he throw himself in?

Answer.—Well, say you don't know Gaspard. He will pause irresolute up to the limit, then, with a fierce struggle, will recall his courage and hasten from the Bridge.

Question.—This struggle not to throw oneself in must be dreadfully difficult?

Answer.—Oh! dreadfully! Most of us are so frail we should jump in at once. But Gaspard has the knack of it. Besides he still has some of the Sheik's herb; he chews it.

Question.—What has happened to De Vaux anyway? Is it anything he has eaten?

Answer.—No, it is nothing that he has eaten. It's about her. The blow has come. She has no use for sunburn, doesn't care for tan; she is going to marry a duke and the boy lieutenant is no longer in it. The real trouble is that the modern novelist has got beyond the happy-marriage mode of ending. He wants tragedy and a blighted life to wind up with.

Question.—How will the book conclude?

Answer.—Oh, De Vaux will go back to the desert, fall upon the Sheik's neck, and swear to be a second Hairy

Hank to him. There will be a final panorama of the desert, the Sheik and his newly found son at the door of the tent, the sun setting behind a pyramid, and De Vaux's faithful elephant crouched at his feet and gazing up at him with dumb affection.

HELPING THE ARMENIANS

THE financial affairs of the parish church up at Doogalville have been getting rather into a tangle in the last six months. The people of the church were specially anxious to do something toward the general public subscription of the town on behalf of the unhappy Armenians, and to that purpose they determined to devote the collections taken up at a series of special evening services. To give the right sort of swing to the services and to stimulate generous giving, they put a new pipe organ into the church. In order to make a preliminary payment on the organ, it was decided to raise a mortgage on the parsonage.

To pay the interest on the mortgage, the choir of the church got up a sacred concert in the town hall.

To pay for the town hall, the Willing Workers' Guild held a social in the Sunday school. To pay the expenses of the social, the rector delivered a public lecture on "Italy and Her Past," illustrated by a magic lantern. To pay for the magic lantern, the curate and the ladies of the church got up some amateur theatricals.

Finally, to pay for the costumes for the theatricals, the rector felt it his duty to dispense with the curate.

So that is where the church stands just at present. What

they chiefly want to do, is to raise enough money to buy a suitable gold watch as a testimonial to the curate. After that they hope to be able to do something for the Armenians. Meantime, of course, the Armenians, the ones right there in the town, are getting very troublesome. To begin with, there is the Armenian who rented the costumes for the theatricals: he has to be squared. Then there is the Armenian organ dealer, and the Armenian who owned the magic lantern. They want relief badly.

The most urgent case is that of the Armenian who holds the mortgage on the parsonage; indeed it is generally felt in the congregation, when the rector makes his impassioned appeals at the special services on behalf of the suffering cause, that it is to this man that he has special reference.

In the meanwhile, the general public subscription is not getting along very fast; but the proprietor of the big saloon further down the street and the man with the short cigar that runs the Doogalville Midway Plaisance have been most liberal in their contributions.

A STUDY IN STILL LIFE —THE COUNTRY HOTEL

THE country hotel stands on the sunny side of Main Street. It has three entrances.

There is one in front which leads into the Bar. There is one at the side called the Ladies' Entrance which leads into the Bar from the side. There is also the Main Entrance which leads into the Bar through the Rotunda.

The Rotunda is the space between the door of the bar-room and the cigar-case.

In it is a desk and a book. In the book are written down the names of the guests, together with marks indicating the direction of the wind and the height of the barometer. It is here that the newly arrived guest waits until he has time to open the door leading to the Bar.

The bar-room forms the largest part of the hotel. It constitutes the hotel proper. To it are attached a series of bedrooms on the floor above, many of which contain beds.

The walls of the bar-room are perforated in all directions with trap-doors. Through one of these, drinks are passed into the back sitting-room. Through others drinks are passed into the passages. Drinks are also passed through the floor and through the ceiling. Drinks once passed never return. The Proprietor stands in the doorway of the Bar. He weighs two hundred pounds. His face is immovable as putty. He is drunk. He has been drunk for twelve years. It makes no difference to him. Behind the Bar stands the Bar-tender. He wears wicker-sleeves, his hair is curled in a hook, and his name is Charlie.

Attached to the Bar is a pneumatic beer-pump, by means of which the Bar-tender can flood the Bar with beer. Afterwards he wipes up the beer with a rag. By this means he polishes the Bar. Some of the beer that is pumped up spills into glasses and has to be sold.

Behind the Bar-tender is a mechanism called a cash-register, which, on being struck a powerful blow, rings a bell, sticks up a card marked NO SALE, and opens a till from which the Bar-tender distributes money.

There is printed a tariff of drinks and prices on the wall.

It reads thus:

Beer	5 cents.
Whisky	5 cents.
Whisky and Soda . . .	5 cents.
Beer and Soda . . .	5 cents.
Whisky and Beer and Soda . .	5 cents.
Whisky and Eggs . . .	5 cents.
Beer and Eggs . . .	5 cents.
Champagne . . .	5 cents.
Cigars	5 cents.
Cigars, extra fine . . .	5 cents.

All calculations are made on this basis and are worked out to three places of decimals. Every seventh drink is on the house and is not followed by a distribution of money.

The bar-room closes at midnight, provided there are enough people in it. If there is not a quorum the Proprietor waits for a better chance. A careful closing of the Bar will often catch as many as twenty-five people. The Bar is not opened again till seven o'clock in the morning; after that the people may go home. There are also, nowadays, Local Option Hotels. These contain only one entrance, leading directly into the Bar.

AN EXPERIMENT WITH POLICEMAN HOGAN

MR. SCALPER sits writing in the reporters' room of *The Daily Eclipse*. The paper has gone to press and he is alone; a wayward talented gentleman, this Mr. Scalper, and employed by *The Eclipse* as a delineator of character from handwriting. Any subscriber who forwards a specimen of his handwriting is treated to a prompt analysis of his character from Mr. Scalper's facile pen. The literary genius has a little pile of correspondence beside him, and is engaged in the practice of his art. Outside the night is dark and rainy. The clock on the City Hall marks the hour of two. In front of the newspaper office Policeman Hogan walks drearily up and down his beat. The damp misery of Hogan is intense. A belated gentleman in clerical attire, returning home from a bed of sickness, gives him a side-look of timid pity and shivers past. Hogan follows the retreating figure with his eye; then draws forth a notebook and sits down on the steps of *The Eclipse* building to write in the light of the gas lamp. Gentlemen of nocturnal habits have often wondered what it is that Policeman Hogan and his brethren write in their little books. Here are the words that are fashioned by the big fist of the policeman.

"Two o'clock. All is well. There is a light in Mr. Scalper's room above. The night is very wet and I am unhappy and cannot sleep—my fourth night of insomnia. Suspicious-looking individual just passed. Alas, how melancholy is my life! Will the dawn never break! Oh, moist, moist stone."

Mr. Scalper up above is writing too, writing with the careless fluency of a man who draws his pay by the column. He is delineating with skill and rapidity. The reporters' room is gloomy and desolate. Mr. Scalper is a man of sensitive temperament and the dreariness of his surroundings depresses him. He opens the letter of a correspondent, examines the handwriting narrowly, casts his eye around the room for inspiration, and proceeds to delineate:

"G.H. You have an unhappy, despondent nature:

your circumstances oppress you, and your life is filled with an infinite sadness. You feel that you are without hope——"

Mr. Scalper pauses, takes another look around the room, and finally lets his eye rest for some time upon a tall black bottle that stands on the shelf of an open cupboard. Then he goes on:

"—and you have lost all belief in Christianity and a future world and human virtue. You are very weak against temptation, but there is an ugly vein of determination in your character, when you make up your mind that you are going to have a thing——"

Here Mr. Scalper stops abruptly, pushes back his chair, and dashes across the room to the cupboard. He takes the black bottle from the shelf, applies it to his lips, and remains for some time motionless. He then returns to finish the delineation of G.H. with the hurried words:

"On the whole I recommend you to persevere; you are doing very well." Mr. Scalper's next proceeding is peculiar. He takes from the cupboard a roll of twine, about fifty feet in length, and attaches one end of it to the neck of the bottle. Going then to one of the windows, he opens it, leans out, and whistles softly. The alert ear of Policeman Hogan on the pavement below catches the sound, and he returns it. The bottle is lowered to the end of the string, the guardian of the peace applies it to his gullet, and for some time the policeman and the man of letters remain attached by a cord of sympathy. Gentlemen who lead the variegated life of Mr. Scalper find it well to propitiate the arm of the law, and attachments of this sort are not uncommon. Mr. Scalper hauls up the bottle, closes the window, and returns to his task; the policeman resumes his walk with a glow of internal satisfaction. A glance at the City Hall clock causes him to enter another note in his book.

"Half-past two. All is better. The weather is milder with a feeling of young summer in the air. Two lights in Mr. Scalper's room. Nothing has occurred which need be brought to the notice of the roundsman."

Things are going better upstairs too. The delineator opens a second envelope, surveys the writing of the correspondent with a critical yet charitable eye, and writes with more complacency.

"William H. Your writing shows a disposition which, though naturally melancholy, is capable of a temporary cheerfulness. You have known misfortune but have made up your mind to look on the bright side of things. If you will allow me to say so, you indulge in liquor but are quite moderate in your use of it. Be assured that no harm ever comes of this moderate use. It enlivens the intellect, brightens the faculties, and stimulates the dormant fancy into a pleasurable activity. It is only when carried to excess——"

At this point the feelings of Mr. Scalper, who had been writing very rapidly, evidently become too much for him. He starts up from his chair, rushes two or three times around the room, and finally returns to finish the delineation thus: "it is only when carried to excess that this moderation becomes pernicious."

Mr. Scalper succumbs to the train of thought suggested and gives an illustration of how moderation to excess may be avoided, after which he lowers the bottle to Policeman Hogan with a cheery exchange of greetings.

The half-hours pass on. The delineator is writing busily and feels that he is writing well. The characters of his correspondents lie bare to his keen eye and flow from his facile pen. From time to time he pauses and appeals to the source of his inspiration; his humanity prompts him to extend the inspiration to Policeman Hogan. The minion of the law walks his beat with a feeling of more than tranquillity. A solitary Chinaman, returning home late from his midnight laundry, scuttles past. The literary instinct has risen strong in Hogan from his connection with the man of genius above him, and the passage of the lone Chinee gives him occasion to write in his book.

"Four-thirty. Everything is simply great. There are four lights in Mr. Scalper's room. Mild, balmy weather with prospects of an earthquake, which may be held in check by walking with extreme caution. Two Chinamen have just passed—mandarins, I presume. Their walk was unsteady, but their faces so benign as to disarm suspicion."

Up in the office Mr. Scalper has reached the letter of a correspondent which appears to give him particular pleasure, for he delineates the character with a beaming smile of satisfaction. To the unpractised eye the writing resembles the prim, angular hand of an elderly spinster. Mr. Scalper, however, seems to think otherwise, for he writes:

"Aunt Dorothea. You have a merry, rollicking nature. At times you are seized with a wild tumultuous hilarity to which you give ample vent in shouting and song. You are much addicted to profanity, and you rightly feel that this is part of your nature and you must not check it. The world is a very bright place to you, Aunt Dorothea. Write to me again soon. Our minds seem cast in the same mould."

Mr. Scalper seems to think that he has not done full justice to the subject he is treating, for he proceeds to write a long private letter to Aunt Dorothea in addition to the printed delineation. As he finishes the City Hall clock points to five, and Policeman Hogan makes the last entry in his chronicle. Hogan has seated himself upon the steps of *The Eclipse* building for greater comfort and writes with a slow, leisurely fist:

"The other hand of the clock points north and the second longest points south-east by south. I infer that it is five o'clock. The electric lights in Mr. Scalper's room defy the eye. The roundsman has passed and examined my notes of the night's occurrences. They are entirely satisfactory, and he is pleased with their literary form. The earthquake which I apprehended was reduced to a few minor oscillations which cannot reach me where I sit——"

The lowering of the bottle interrupts Policeman Hogan. The long letter to Aunt Dorothea has cooled the ardour of Mr. Scalper. The generous blush has passed from his mind and he has been trying in vain to restore it. To afford Hogan a similar opportunity, he decides not to haul the bottle up immediately, but to leave it in his custody while he delineates a character. The writing of this correspondent would seem to the inexperienced eye to be that of a timid little maiden in her teens. Mr. Scalper is not to be deceived by appearances. He shakes his head mournfully at the letter and writes:

"Little Emily. You have known great happiness, but it has passed. Despondency has driven you to seek forgetfulness in drink. Your writing shows the worst phase of the liquor habit. I apprehend that you will shortly have delirium tremens. Poor little Emily! Do not try to break off; it is too late."

Mr. Scalper is visibly affected by his correspondent's unhappy condition. His eye becomes moist, and he decides to haul up the bottle while there is still time to save Policeman Hogan from acquiring a taste for liquor. He is surprised and alarmed to find the attempt to haul it up ineffectual. The minion of the law has fallen into a leaden slumber, and the bottle remains tight in his grasp. The baffled delineator lets fall the string and returns to finish his task. Only a few lines are now required to fill the column, but Mr. Scalper finds on examining the correspondence that he has exhausted the subjects. This, however, is quite a common occurrence and occasions no dilemma in the mind of the talented gentleman. It is his custom in such cases to fill up the space with an imaginary character or two, the analysis of which is a task most congenial to his mind. He bows his head in thought for a few moments, and then writes as follows:

"Policeman H. Your hand shows great firmness; when once set upon a thing you are not easily moved. But you have a mean, grasping disposition and a tendency to want more than your share. You have formed an attachment which you hope will be continued throughout life, but your selfishness threatens to sever the bond."

Having written which, Mr. Scalper arranges his manuscript for the printer next day, dons his hat and coat, and wends his way home in the morning twilight, feeling that his pay is earned.

THE PASSING OF THE POET

STUDIES in what may be termed collective psychology are essentially in keeping with the spirit of the present century. The examination of the mental tendencies, the intellectual habits which we display not as individuals, but as members of a race, community, or crowd, is offering a fruitful field of speculation as yet but little exploited. One may, therefore, not without profit, pass in review the relation of the poetic instinct to the intellectual development of the present era.

Not the least noticeable feature in the psychological evolution of our time is the rapid disappearance of poetry. The art of writing poetry, or perhaps more fairly, the habit of writing poetry, is passing from us. The poet is destined to become extinct.

To a reader of trained intellect the initial difficulty at once suggests itself as to what is meant by poetry. But it is needless to quibble at a definition of the term. It may be designated, simply and fairly, as the art of expressing a simple truth in a concealed form of words, any number of which, at intervals greater or less, may or may not rhyme.

The poet, it must be said, is as old as civilisation. The Greeks had him with them, stamping out his iambics with the sole of his foot. The Romans, too, knew him—endlessly juggling his syllables together, long and short, short and long, to make hexameters. This can now be done by electricity, but the Romans did not know it.

But it is not my present purpose to speak of the poets

of an earlier and ruder time. For the subject before us it is enough to set our age in comparison with the era that preceded it. We have but to contrast ourselves with our early Victorian grandfathers to realise the profound revolution that has taken place in public feeling. It is only with an effort that the practical common sense of the twentieth century can realise the excessive sentimentality of the earlier generation.

In those days poetry stood in high and universal esteem. Parents read poetry to their children. Children recited poetry to their parents. And he was a dullard, indeed, who did not at least profess, in his hours of idleness, to pour spontaneous rhythm from his flowing quill.

Should one gather statistics of the enormous production of poetry some sixty or seventy years ago, they would scarcely appear credible. Journals and magazines teemed with it. Editors openly countenanced it. Even the daily press affected it. Love sighed in home-made stanzas. Patriotism rhapsodised on the hustings, or cited rolling hexameters to an enraptured legislature. Even melancholy death courted his everlasting sleep in elegant elegiacs.

In that era, indeed, I know not how, polite society was haunted by the obstinate fiction that it was the duty of a man of parts to express himself from time to time in verse. Any special occasion of expansion or exuberance, of depression, torsion, or introspection, was sufficient to call it forth. So we have poems of dejection, of reflection, of deglutition, of indigestion.

Any particular psychological disturbance was enough to provoke an excess of poetry. The character and manner of the verse might vary with the predisposing cause. A gentleman who had dined too freely might disexpand himself in a short fit of lyric doggerel in which "bowl" and "soul" were freely rhymed. The morning's indigestion inspired a long-drawn elegiac, with "bier" and "tear," "mortal" and "portal" linked in sonorous sadness. The man of politics, from time to time, grateful to an appreciative country, sang back to it, "Ho, Albion, rising from the brine!" in verse whose intention at least was meritorious.

And yet it was but a fiction, a purely fictitious obligation, self-imposed by a sentimental society. In plain truth, poetry came no more easily or naturally to the early Victorian than to you or me. The lover twanged his obdurate harp in vain for hours for the rhymes that would not come, and the man of politics hammered at his heavy hexameter long indeed before his Albion was finally "hoed" into shape; while the beer-besotted convivialist cudgelled his poor wits cold sober in rhyming the light little bottle-ditty that should have sprung like Aphrodite from the froth of the champagne.

I have before me a pathetic witness of this fact. It is the note-book once used for the random jottings of a gentleman of the period. In it I read: "Fair Lydia, if my earthly harp." This is crossed out, and below it appears, "Fair Lydia, COULD my earthly harp." This again is erased, and under it appears, "FAIR LYDIA, should my earthly harp." This again is struck out with a despairing stroke, and amended to read: "Fair Lydia, DID my earthly harp." So that finally, when the lines appeared in the *Gentleman's Magazine* (1845) in their ultimate shape—"Fair Edith, when with fluent pen," etc., etc.—one can realise from what a desperate congelation the fluent pen had been so perseveringly rescued.

There can be little doubt of the deleterious effect

occasioned both to public and private morals by this deliberate exaltation of mental susceptibility on the part of the early Victorian. In many cases we can detect the evidences of incipient paresis. The undue access of emotion frequently assumed a pathological character. The sight of a daisy, of a withered leaf or an upturned sod, seemed to disturb the poet's mental equipoise. Spring unnerved him. The lambs distressed him. The flowers made him cry. The daffodils made him laugh. Day dazzled him. Night frightened him.

This exalted mood, combined with the man's culpable ignorance of the plainest principles of physical science, made him see something out of the ordinary in the flight of a waterfowl or the song of a skylark. He complained that he could *hear* it, but not *see* it—a phenomenon too familiar to the scientific observer to occasion any comment.

In such a state of mind the most inconsequential inferences were drawn. One said that the brightness of the dawn—a fact easily explained by the diurnal motion of the globe—showed him that his soul was immortal. He asserted further that he had, at an earlier period of his life, trailed bright clouds behind him. This was absurd.

With the disturbance thus set up in the nervous system were coupled, in many instances, mental aberrations, particularly in regard to pecuniary matters. "Give me not silk, nor rich attire," pleaded one poet of the period to the British public, "nor gold nor jewels rare." Here was an evident hallucination that the writer was to become the recipient of an enormous secret subscription. Indeed, the earnest desire NOT to be given gold was a recurrent characteristic of the poetic temperament. The repugnance to accept even a handful of gold was generally accompanied by a desire for a draught of pure water or a night's rest.

It is pleasing to turn from this excessive sentimentality of thought and speech to the practical and concise diction of our time. We have learned to express ourselves with equal force, but greater simplicity. To illustrate this I have gathered from the poets of the earlier generation and from the prose writers of today parallel passages that may be fairly set in contrast. Here, for example, is a passage from the poet Grey, still familiar to scholars:

> "Can storied urn or animated bust
> Back to its mansion call the fleeting breath?
> Can honour's voice invoke the silent dust
> Or flattery soothe the dull cold ear of death?"

Precisely similar in thought, though different in form, is the more modern presentation found in Huxley's *Physiology*:

"Whether after the moment of death the ventricles of the heart can be again set in movement by the artificial stimulus of oxygen, is a question to which we must impose a decided negative."

How much simpler, and yet how far superior to Grey's elaborate phraseology! Huxley has here seized the central point of the poet's thought, and expressed it with the dignity and precision of exact science.

I cannot refrain, even at the risk of needless iteration, from quoting a further example. It is taken from the poet Burns. The original dialect, being written in inverted hiccoughs, is rather difficult to reproduce. It describes the scene attendant upon the return of a cottage labourer to his home on Saturday night:

"The cheerfu' supper done, wi' serious face
They round the ingle form in a circle wide;
The sire turns o'er, wi' patriarchal grace,
The big ha' Bible, ance his father's pride:
His bonnet rev'rently is laid aside,
His lyart haffets wearing thin an' bare:
Those strains that once did sweet in Zion glide,
He wales a portion wi' judeecious care."

Now I find almost the same scene described in more apt phraseology in the police news of the *Dumfries Chronicle* (October 3, 1909), thus: "It appears that the prisoner had returned to his domicile at the usual hour, and, after partaking of a hearty meal, had seated himself on his oaken settle, for the ostensible purpose of reading the Bible. It was while so occupied that his arrest was effected." With the trifling exception that Burns omits all mention of the arrest, for which, however, the whole tenor of the poem gives ample warrant, the two accounts are almost identical.

In all that I have thus said I do not wish to be misunderstood. Believing, as I firmly do, that the poet is destined to become extinct, I am not one of those who would accelerate his extinction. The time has not yet come for remedial legislation, or the application of the criminal law. Even in obstinate cases where pronounced delusions in reference to plants, animals, and natural phenomena are seen to exist, it is better that we should do nothing that might occasion a mistaken remorse. The inevitable natural evolution which is thus shaping the mould of human thought may safely be left to its own course.

SELF-MADE MEN

THEY were both what we commonly call successful business-men—men with well-fed faces, heavy signet rings on fingers like sausages, and broad, comfortable waistcoats, a yard and a half round the equator. They were seated opposite each other at a table of a first-class restaurant, and had fallen into conversation while waiting to give their order to the waiter. Their talk had drifted back to their early days and how each had made his start in life when he first struck New York.

"I tell you what, Jones," one of them was saying, "I shall never forget my first few years in this town. By George, it was pretty uphill work! Do you know, sir, when I first struck this place, I hadn't more than fifteen cents to my name, hadn't a rag except what I stood up in, and all the place I had to sleep in—you won't believe it, but it's a gospel fact just the same—was an empty tar barrel. No, sir," he went on, leaning back and closing up his eyes into an expression of infinite experience, "no, sir, a fellow accustomed to luxury like you has simply no idea what sleeping out in a tar barrel and all that kind of thing is like."

"My dear Robinson," the other man rejoined briskly "if you imagine I've had no experience of hardship of that sort, you never made a bigger mistake in your life Why, when I first walked into this town I hadn't a cent, sir, not a cent, and as for lodging, all the place I had for months and months was an old piano box up a lane, behind a factory. Talk about hardship, I guess I had it pretty rough! You take a fellow that's used to a good warm tar barrel and put him into a piano box for a night or two, and you'll see mighty soon——"

"My dear fellow," Robinson broke in with some irritation, "you merely show that you don't know what a tar barrel's like. Why, on winter nights, when you'd be shut in there in your piano box just as snug as you please, I used to lie awake shivering, with the draught fairly running in at the bunghole at the back."

"Draught!" sneered the other man, with a provoking laugh, "draught! Don't talk to me about draughts. This box I speak of had a whole darned plank right off it, right on the north side too. I used to sit there studying in the evenings, and the snow would blow in a foot deep. And yet, sir," he continued more quietly, "though I know you'll not believe it, I don't mind admitting that some of the happiest days of my life were spent in that same old box. Ah, those were good old times! Bright, innocent days, I can tell you. I'd wake up there in the mornings and fairly shout with high spirits. Of course, you may not be able to stand that kind of life——"

"Not stand it!" cried Robinson fiercely; "me not stand it! By gad! I'm made for it. I just wish I had a taste of the old life again for a while. And as for innocence! Well, I'll bet you you weren't one-tenth as innocent as I was; no, nor one-fifth, nor one-third! What a grand old life it was! You'll swear this is a darned lie and refuse to believe it—but I can remember evenings when I'd have two or three fellows in, and we'd sit round and play pedro by a candle half the night."

"Two or three!" laughed Jones; "why, my dear fellow, I've known half a dozen of us to sit down to supper in my piano box, and have a game of pedro afterwards; yes, and charades and forfeits, and every other darned thing. Mighty good suppers they were too!

By Jove, Robinson, you fellows round this town who have ruined your digestions with high living, have no notion of the zest with which a man can sit down to a few potato peelings, or a bit of broken pie crust, or——"

"Talk about hard food," interrupted the other, "I guess I know all about that. Many's the time I've breakfasted off a little cold porridge that somebody was going to throw away from a back-door, or that I've gone round to a livery stable and begged a little bran mash that they intended for the pigs. I'll venture to say I've eaten more hog's food——"

"Hog's food!" shouted Robinson, striking his fist savagely on the table, "I tell you hog's food suits me better than——"

He stopped speaking with a sudden grunt of surprise as the waiter appeared with the question:

"What may I bring you for dinner, gentlemen?"

"Dinner!" said Jones, after a moment of silence, "dinner! Oh, anything, nothing—I never care what I eat—give me a little cold porridge, if you've got it, or a chunk of salt pork—anything you like, it's all the same to me."

The waiter turned with an impassive face to Robinson.

"You can bring me some of that cold porridge too," he said, with a defiant look at Jones; "yesterday's, if you have it, and a few potato peelings and a glass of skim milk."

There was a pause. Jones sat back in his chair and looked hard across at Robinson. For some moments the two men gazed into each other's eyes with a stern, defiant intensity. Then Robinson turned slowly round in his seat and beckoned to the waiter, who was moving off with the muttered order on his lips.

"Here, waiter," he said with a savage scowl, "I guess

I'll change that order a little. Instead of that cold porridge I'll take—um, yes—a little hot partridge. And you might as well bring me an oyster or two on the half shell, and a mouthful of soup (mock-turtle, consommé, anything), and perhaps you might fetch along a dab of fish, and a little peck of Stilton, and a grape, or a walnut."

The waiter turned to Jones.

"I guess I'll take the same," he said simply, and added, "and you might bring a quart of champagne at the same time."

And nowadays, when Jones and Robinson meet, the memory of the tar barrel and the piano box is buried as far out of sight as a home for the blind under a landslide.

A MODEL DIALOGUE

In which is shown how the drawing-room juggler may be permanently cured of his card trick.

The drawing-room juggler, having slyly got hold of the pack of cards at the end of the game of whist, says:

"Ever see any card tricks? Here's rather a good one; pick a card."

"Thank you, I don't want a card."

"No, but just pick one, any one you like, and I'll tell which one you pick."

"You'll tell who?"

"No, no; I mean, I'll know which it is, don't you see? Go on now, pick a card."

"Any one I like?"

"Yes."

"Any colour at all?"

"Yes, yes."

"Any suit?"

"Oh, yes; do go on."

"Well, let me see, I'll—pick—the—ace—of—spades."

"Great Cæsar! I mean you are to pull a card out of the pack."

"Oh, to pull it out of the pack! Now I understand. Hand me the pack. All right—I've got it."

"Have you picked one?"

"Yes, it's the three of hearts. Did you know it?"

"Hang it! Don't tell me like that. You spoil the thing. Here, try again. Pick a card."

"All right, I've got it."

"Put it back in the pack. Thanks. (Shuffle, shuffle, shuffle—flip)—There, is that it?" (triumphantly).

"I don't know. I lost sight of it."

"Lost sight of it! Confound it, you have to look at it and see what it is."

"Oh, you want me to look at the front of it!"

"Why, of course! Now then, pick a card."

"All right. I've picked it. Go ahead." (Shuffle, shuffle, shuffle—flip.)

"Say, confound you, did you put that card back in the pack?"

"Why, no. I kept it."

"Holy Moses! Listen. Pick—a—card—just one—look at it—see what it is—then put it back—do you understand?"

"Oh, perfectly. Only I don't see how you are ever going to do it. You must be awfully clever."

(Shuffle, shuffle, shuffle—flip.)

"There you are; that's your card, now, isn't it?" (This is the supreme moment.)

"NO. THAT IS NOT MY CARD." (This is a flat lie, but Heaven will pardon you for it.)

"Not that card ! ! ! ! Say—just hold on a second. Here, now, watch what you're at this time. I can do this cursed thing, mind you, every time. I've done it on father, on mother, and on every one that's ever come round our place. Pick a card. (Shuffle, shuffle, shuffle—flip, bang.) There, that's your card."

"NO. I AM SORRY. THAT IS NOT MY CARD. But won't you try it again? Please do. Perhaps you are a little excited—I'm afraid I was rather stupid. Won't you go and sit quietly by yourself on the back verandah for half an hour and then try? You have to go home? Oh, I'm so sorry. It must be such an awfully clever little trick. Good night!"

BACK TO THE BUSH

I HAVE a friend called Billy who has the Bush Mania. By trade he is a doctor, but I do not think that he needs to sleep out of doors. In ordinary things his mind appears sound. Over the tops of his gold-rimmed spectacles, as he bends forward to speak to you, there gleams nothing but amiability and kindliness. Like all the rest of us he is, or was until he forgot it all, an extremely well-educated man.

I am aware of no criminal strain in his blood. Yet Billy is in reality hopelessly unbalanced. He has the Mania of the Open Woods.

Worse than that, he is haunted with the desire to drag his friends with him into the depths of the Bush.

Whenever we meet he starts to talk about it.

Not long ago I met him in the club.

"I wish," he said, "you'd let me take you clear away up the Gatineau."

"Yes, I wish I would, I don't think," I murmured to myself, but I humoured him and said:

"How do we go, Billy, in a motor-car or by train?"

"No, we paddle."

"And is it up-stream all the way?"

"Oh, yes," Billy said enthusiastically.

"And how many days do we paddle all day to get up?"

"Six."

"Couldn't we do it in less?"

"Yes," Billy answered, feeling that I was entering into the spirit of the thing, "if we start each morning just before daylight and paddle hard till moonlight, we could do it in five days and a half."

"Glorious! and are there portages?"

"Lots of them."

"And at each of these do I carry two hundred pounds of stuff up a hill on my back?"

"Yes."

"And will there be a guide, a genuine, dirty-looking Indian guide?"

"Yes."

"And can I sleep next to him?"

"Oh, yes, if you want to."

"And when we get to the top, what is there?"

"Well, we go over the height of land."

"Oh, we do, do we? And is the height of land all rock and about three hundred yards up-hill? And do I carry a barrel of flour up it? And does it roll down and crush me on the other side? Look here, Billy, this trip is a great thing, but it is too luxurious for me. If you will have me paddled up the river in a large iron canoe with an awning, carried over the portages in a sedan-chair, taken across the height of land in a palanquin or a howdah, and lowered down the other side in a derrick, I'll go. Short of that, the thing would be too fattening."

Billy was discouraged and left me. But he has since returned repeatedly to the attack.

He offers to take me to the head-waters of the Batiscan. I am content at the foot.

He wants us to go to the sources of the Attahwapiscat. I don't.

He says I ought to see the grand chutes of the Kewakasis. Why should I?

I have made Billy a counter-proposition that he strike through the Adirondacks (in the train) to New York, from there portage to Atlantic City, then to Washington, carrying our own grub (in the dining-car), camp there a few days (at the Willard), and then back, I to return by train and Billy on foot with the outfit.

The thing is still unsettled.

Billy, of course, is only one of thousands that have got this mania. And the autumn is the time when it rages at its worst.

Every day there move northward trains, packed full of lawyers, bankers, and brokers, headed for the bush. They are dressed up to look like pirates. They wear slouch hats, flannel shirts, and leather breeches with belts. They could afford much better clothes than these, but they won't use them. I don't know where they get these clothes. I think the railroad lends them out. They have guns between their knees and big knives at their hips. They smoke the worst tobacco they can find, and they carry ten gallons of alcohol per man in the baggage car.

In the intervals of telling lies to one another they read the railroad pamphlets about hunting. This kind of literature is deliberately and fiendishly contrived to infuriate their mania. I know all about these pamphlets because I write them. I once, for instance, wrote up, from imagination, a little place called Dog Lake at the end of a branch line. The place had failed as a settlement, and the railroad had decided to turn it into a hunting resort. I did the turning. I think I did it rather well, rechristening the lake and stocking the place with suitable varieties of game. The pamphlet ran like this.

"The limpid waters of Lake Owatawetness (the name, according to the old Indian legends of the place, signifies, The Mirror of the Almighty) abound with every known variety of fish. Near to its surface, so close that the angler may reach out his hand and stroke them, schools of pike, pickerel, mackerel, doggerel, and chickerel jostle one another in the water. They rise instantaneously to the bait and swim gratefully ashore holding it in their mouths. In the middle depth of the waters of the lake, the sardine, the lobster, the kippered herring, the anchovy and other tinned varieties of fish disport themselves with evident gratification, while even lower in the pellucid depths the dog-fish, the hog-fish, the log-fish, and the sword-fish whirl about in never-ending circles.

"Nor is Lake Owatawetness merely an Angler's Paradise. Vast forests of primeval pine slope to the very shores of the lake, to which descend great droves of bears —brown, green, and bear-coloured—while as the shades of evening fall, the air is loud with the lowing of moose, cariboo, antelope, cantelope, musk-oxes, musk-rats, and other graminivorous mammalia of the forest. These enormous quadrumana generally move off about 10.30

p.m., from which hour until 11.45 p.m. the whole shore is reserved for bison and buffalo.

"After midnight hunters who so desire it can be chased through the woods, for any distance and at any speed they select, by jaguars, panthers, cougars, tigers, and jackals whose ferocity is reputed to be such that they will tear the breeches off a man with their teeth in their eagerness to sink their fangs in his palpitating flesh. Hunters, attention! Do not miss such attractions as these!"

I have seen men—quiet, reputable, well-shaved men—reading that pamphlet of mine in the rotundas of hotels, with their eyes blazing with excitement. I think it is the jaguar attraction that hits them the hardest, because I notice them rub themselves sympathetically with their hands while they read.

Of course, you can imagine the effect of this sort of literature on the brains of men fresh from their offices, and dressed out as pirates.

They just go crazy and stay crazy.

Just watch them when they get into the bush.

Notice that well-to-do stockbroker crawling about on his stomach in the underbrush, with his spectacles shining like gig-lamps. What is he doing? He is after a cariboo that isn't there. He is "stalking" it. With his stomach. Of course, away down in his heart he knows that the cariboo isn't there and never was; but that man read my pamphlet and went crazy. He can't help it: he's *got* to stalk something. Mark him as he crawls along; see him crawl through a thimbleberry bush (very quietly so that the cariboo won't hear the noise of the prickles going into him), then through a bee's nest, gently and slowly, so that the cariboo will not take fright when the bees are stinging him. Sheer woodcraft! Yes, mark him. Mark him in any way you like. Go up behind him and paint a blue cross on the seat of his pants as he crawls. He'll never notice. He thinks he's a hunting-dog. Yet this is the man who laughs at his little son of ten for crawling round under the dining-room table with a mat over his shoulders, and pretending to be a bear.

Now see these other men in camp.

Someone has told them—I think I first started the idea in my pamphlet—that the thing is to sleep on a pile of hemlock branches. I think I told them to listen to the wind sowing (you know the word I mean), sowing and crooning in the giant pines. So there they are upside down, doubled up on a couch of green spikes that would have killed St. Sebastian. They stare up at the sky with blood-shot, restless eyes, waiting for the crooning to begin. And there isn't a sow in sight.

Here is another man, ragged and with a six days' growth of beard, frying a piece of bacon on a stick over a little fire. Now what does he think he is? The *chef* of the Waldorf Astoria? Yes, he does, and what's more he thinks that that miserable bit of bacon, cut with a tobacco knife from a chunk of meat that lay six days in the rain, is fit to eat. What's more, he'll eat it. So will the rest. They're all crazy together.

There's another man, the Lord help him, who thinks he has the "knack" of being a carpenter. He is hammering up shelves to a tree. Till the shelves fall down he thinks he is a wizard. Yet this is the same man who swore at his wife for asking him to put up a shelf in the back kitchen. "How the blazes," he asked, "could he nail the damn thing up? Did she think he was a plumber?"

After all, never mind.

Provided they are happy up there, let them stay.

Personally, I wouldn't mind if they didn't come back

and lie about it. They get back to the city dead fagged for want of sleep, sogged with alcohol, bitten brown by the bush-flies, trampled on by the moose, and chased through the brush by bears and skunks—and they have the nerve to say that they like it.

Sometimes I think they do.

Men are only animals anyway. They like to get out into the woods and growl round at night and feel something bite them.

Only why haven't they the imagination to be able to do the same thing with less fuss? Why not take their coats and collars off in the office and crawl round on the floor and growl at one another. It would be just as good.

REFLECTIONS ON RIDING

THE writing of this paper has been inspired by a debate recently held at the literary society of my native town on the question, "Resolved: that the bicycle is a nobler animal than the horse." In order to speak for the negative with proper authority, I have spent some weeks in completely addicting myself to the use of the horse. I find that the difference between the horse and the bicycle is greater than I had supposed.

The horse is entirely covered with hair; the bicycle is not entirely covered with hair, except the '89 model they are using in Idaho.

In riding a horse the performer finds that the pedals in which he puts his feet will not allow of a good circular stroke. He will observe, however, that there is a saddle in which—especially while the horse is trotting—he is expected to seat himself from time to time. But it is simpler to ride standing up, with the feet in the pedals.

There are no handles to a horse, but the 1910 model has a string to each side of its face for turning its head when there is anything you want it to see.

Coasting on a good horse is superb, but should be under control. I have known a horse to suddenly begin to coast with me about two miles from home, coast down the main street of my native town at a terrific rate, and finally coast through a platoon of the Salvation Army into its livery stable.

I cannot honestly deny that it takes a good deal of physical courage to ride a horse. This, however, I have. I get it at about forty cents a flask, and take it as required.

I find that in riding a horse up the long street of a country town, it is not well to proceed at a trot. It excites unkindly comment. It is better to let the horse walk the whole distance. This may be made to seem natural by turning half round in the saddle with the hand on the horse's back, and gazing intently about two miles up the road. It then appears that you are the first in of about fourteen men.

Since learning to ride, I have taken to noticing the things that people do on horse-back in books. Some of these I can manage, but most of them are entirely beyond me. Here, for instance, is a form of equestrian performance that every reader will recognise and for which I have only a despairing admiration:

"With a hasty gesture of farewell, the rider set spurs to his horse and disappeared in a cloud of dust."

With a little practice in the matter of adjustment, I think I could set spurs to any size of horse, but I could never disappear in a cloud of dust—at least, not with any guarantee of remaining disappeared when the dust cleared away.

Here, however, is one that I certainly can do:

"The bridle-rein dropped from Lord Everard's listless hand, and, with his head bowed upon his bosom, he suffered his horse to move at a foot's pace up the sombre avenue. Deep in thought, he heeded not the movement of the steed which bore him."

That is, he looked as if he didn't; but in my case, Lord Everard has his eye on the steed pretty closely, just the same.

This next I am doubtful about:

"To horse! to horse!" cried the knight, and leaped into the saddle.

I think I could manage it if it read:

"To horse!" cried the knight, and, snatching a step-ladder from the hands of his trusty attendant, he rushed into the saddle.

As a concluding remark, I may mention that my experience of riding has thrown a very interesting side-light upon a rather puzzling point in history. It is recorded of the famous Henry the Second that he was "almost constantly in the saddle, and of so restless a disposition that he never sat down, even at meals." I had hitherto been unable to understand Henry's idea about his meals, but I think I can appreciate it now.

SALOONIO

A STUDY IN SHAKESPEAREAN CRITICISM

THEY say that young men fresh from college are pretty positive about what they know. But from my own experience of life, I should say that if you take a comfortable, elderly man who hasn't been near a college for about twenty years, who has been pretty liberally fed and dined ever since, who measures about fifty inches around the circumference, and has a complexion like a cranberry by candlelight, you will find that there is a degree of absolute certainty about what he thinks he knows that will put any young man to shame. I am specially convinced of this from the case of my friend Colonel Hogshead, a portly, choleric gentleman who made a fortune in the cattle-trade out in Wyoming, and who, in his later days, has acquired a chronic idea that the plays of Shakespeare are the one subject upon which he is most qualified to speak personally.

He came across me the other evening as I was sitting by the fire in the club sitting-room looking over the leaves of *The Merchant of Venice,* and began to hold forth to me about the book.

"*Merchant of Venice,* eh? There's a play for you, sir! There's genius! Wonderful, sir, wonderful! You take the characters in that play and where will you find anything like them? You take Antonio, take Sherlock, take Saloonio——"

"Saloonio, Colonel?" I interposed mildly, "aren't you making a mistake? There's a Bassanio and a Salanio in the play, but I don't think there's any Saloonio, is there?"

For a moment Colonel Hogshead's eye became misty with doubt, but he was not the man to admit himself in error:

"Tut, tut! young man," he said with a frown, "don't skim through your books in that way. No Saloonio? Why, of course there's a Saloonio!"

"But I tell you, Colonel," I rejoined, "I've just been reading the play and studying it, and I know there's no such character——"

"Nonsense, sir, nonsense!" said the Colonel, "why he comes in all through; don't tell me, young man, I've read that play myself. Yes, and seen it played, too, out in Wyoming, before you were born, by fellers, sir, that could act. No Saloonio, indeed! why, who is it that is Antonio's friend all through and won't leave him when Bassoonio turns against him? Who rescues Clarissa from Sherlock, and steals the casket of flesh from the Prince of Aragon? Who shouts at the Prince of Morocco, 'Out, out, you damned candlestick'? Who loads up the jury in the trial scene and fixes the doge? No Saloonio! By gad! in my opinion, he's the most important character in the play——"

"Colonel Hogshead," I said very firmly, "there isn't any Saloonio and you know it."

But the old man had got fairly started on whatever dim recollection had given birth to Saloonio; the character seemed to grow more and more luminous in the Colonel's mind, and he continued with increasing animation:

"I'll just tell you what Saloonio is: he's a type. Shakespeare means him to embody the type of the perfect Italian gentleman. He's an idea, that's what he is, he's a symbol, he's a unit——"

Meanwhile I had been searching among the leaves of the play. "Look here," I said, "here's the list of the Dramatis Personæ. There's no Saloonio there."

But this didn't dismay the Colonel one atom. "Why, of course there isn't," he said. "You don't suppose you'd find Saloonio there! That's the whole art of it! That's Shakespeare! That's the whole gist of it! He's kept clean out of the Personæ—gives him scope, gives him a free hand, makes him more of a type than ever. Oh, it's a subtle thing, sir, the dramatic art!" continued the Colonel, subsiding into quiet reflection; "it takes a feller quite a time to get right into Shakespeare's mind and see what he's at all the time."

I began to see that there was no use in arguing any further with the old man. I left him with the idea that the lapse of a little time would soften his views on Saloonio. But I had not reckoned on the way in which old men hang on to a thing. Colonel Hogshead quite took up Saloonio. From that time on Saloonio became the theme of his constant conversation. He was never tired of discussing the character of Saloonio, the wonderful art of the dramatist in creating him, Saloonio's relation to modern life, Saloonio's attitude toward women, the ethical significance of Saloonio, Saloonio as compared with Hamlet, Hamlet as compared with Saloonio—and so on, endlessly. And the more he looked into Saloonio, the more he saw in him.

Saloonio seemed inexhaustible. There were new sides to him—new phases at every turn. The Colonel even read over the play, and finding no mention of Saloonio's name in it, he swore that the books were not the same books they had had out in Wyoming; that the whole part had been cut clean out to suit the book to the infernal public schools, Saloonio's language being—at any rate, as the Colonel quoted it—undoubtedly a trifle free. Then the Colonel took to annotating his book at the side with such remarks as, "Enter Saloonio," or "A tucket sounds; enter Saloonio, on the arm of the Prince of Morocco." When there was no reasonable excuse for bringing Saloonio on the stage the Colonel swore that he was concealed behind the arras, or feasting within with the doge.

But he got satisfaction at last. He had found that there was nobody in our part of the country who knew how to put a play of Shakespeare on the stage, and took a trip to New York to see Sir Henry Irving and Miss Terry do the play. The Colonel sat and listened all through with his face just beaming with satisfaction, and when the curtain fell at the close of Irving's grand presentation of the play, he stood up in his seat and cheered and yelled to his friends: "That's it! That's him! Didn't you see that man that came on the stage all the time and sort of put the whole play through, though you couldn't understand a word he said? Well, that's him! That's Saloonio!"

HALF-HOURS WITH THE POETS

I. MR. WORDSWORTH AND THE LITTLE COTTAGE GIRL

"I met a little cottage girl,
She was eight years old she said
Her hair was thick with many a curl
That clustered round her head."

THIS is what really happened.

Over the dreary downs of his native Cumberland the aged laureate was wandering with bowed head and countenance of sorrow.

Times were bad with the old man.

In the south pocket of his trousers, as he set his face to the north, jingled but a few odd coins and a cheque for St. Leon water. Apparently his cup of bitterness was full.

In the distance a child moved—a child in form, yet the deep lines upon her face bespoke a countenance prematurely old.

The poet espied, pursued and overtook the infant. He observed that apparently she drew her breath lightly and felt her life in every limb, and that presumably her acquaintance with death was of the most superficial character.

"I must sit awhile and ponder on that child," murmured the poet. So he knocked her down with his walking stick and seating himself upon her, he pondered.

Long he sat thus in thought. "His heart is heavy," sighed the child.

At length he drew forth a note-book and pencil and prepared to write upon his knee.

"Now then, my dear young friend," he said, addressing the elfin creature, "I want those lines upon your face. Are you seven?"

"Yes, we are seven," said the girl sadly, and added, "I know what you want. You are going to question me about my afflicted family. You are Mr. Wordsworth, and you are collecting mortuary statistics for the Cottagers' Edition of the Penny Encyclopædia."

"You are eight years old?" asked the bard.

"I suppose so," answered she. "I have been eight years old for years and years."

"And you know nothing of death, of course?" said the poet cheerfully.

"How can I?" answered the child.

"Now then," resumed the venerable William, "let us get to business. Name your brothers and sisters."

"Let me see," began the child wearily; "there was Rube and Ike, two I can't think of, and John and Jane."

"You must not count John and Jane," interrupted the bard reprovingly; "they're dead, you know, so that doesn't make seven."

"I wasn't counting them, but perhaps I added up wrongly," said the child; "and will you please move your overshoe off my neck?"

"Pardon," said the old man. "A nervous trick, I have been absorbed; indeed, the exigency of the metre almost demands my doubling up my feet. To continue, however; which died first?"

"The first to go was little Jane," said the child.

"She lay moaning in bed, I presume?"

"In bed she moaning lay."

"What killed her?"

"Insomnia," answered the girl. "The gaiety of our cottage life, previous to the departure of our elder brothers for Conway, and the constant field-sports in which she indulged with John, proved too much for a frame never too robust."

"You express yourself well," said the poet. "Now, in regard to your unfortunate brother, what was the effect upon him in the following winter of the ground being white with snow and your being able to run and slide?"

"My brother John was forced to go," answered she. "We have been at a loss to understand the cause of his death. We fear that the dazzling glare of the newly fallen snow, acting upon a restless brain, may have led him to a fatal attempt to emulate my own feats upon the ice. And, oh, sir," the child went on, "speak gently of poor Jane. You may rub it into John all you like; we always let him slide."

"Very well," said the bard, "and allow me, in conclusion, one rather delicate question: Do you ever take your little porringer?"

"Oh, yes," answered the child frankly—

> " 'Quite often after sunset,
> When all is light and fair,
> I take my little porringer' —

I can't quite remember what I do after that, but I know that I like it."

"That is immaterial," said Wordsworth. "I can say that you take your little porringer neat, or with bitters, or in water after every meal. As long as I can state that you take a little porringer regularly, but never to excess, the public is satisfied. And now," rising from his seat, "I will not detain you any longer. Here is sixpence—or stay," he added hastily, "here is a cheque for St. Leon water. Your information has been most valuable, and I shall work it, for all I am Wordsworth." With these words the aged poet bowed deferentially to the child and sauntered off in the direction of the Duke of Cumberland's Arms, with his eyes on the ground, as if looking for the meanest flower that blows itself.

II. HOW TENNYSON KILLED THE MAY QUEEN

"If you're waking call me early, call me early, mother dear."

PART I

As soon as the child's malady had declared itself the afflicted parents of the May Queen telegraphed to Tennyson, "Our child gone crazy on subject of early rising, could you come and write some poetry about her?"

Alfred, always prompt to fill orders in writing from the country, came down on the evening train. The old cottager greeted the poet warmly, and began at once to speak of the state of his unfortunate daughter.

"She was took queer in May," he said, "along of a sort of bee that the young folks had; she ain't been just right since; happen you might do summat."

With these words he opened the door of an inner room.

The girl lay in feverish slumber. Beside her bed was an alarm-clock set for half-past three. Connected with the clock was an ingenious arrangement of a falling brick with a string attached to the child's toe.

At the entrance of the visitor she started up in bed.

"Whoop," she yelled, "I am to be Queen of the May, mother, ye-e!"

Then perceiving Tennyson in the doorway, "If that's a caller," she said, "tell him to call me early."

The shock caused the brick to fall. In the subsequent confusion Alfred modestly withdrew to the sitting-room.

"At this rate," he chuckled, "I shall not have long to wait. A few weeks of that strain will finish her."

PART II

Six months had passed.

It was now mid-winter.

And still the girl lived. Her vitality appeared inexhaustible.

She got up earlier and earlier. She now rose yesterday afternoon.

At intervals she seemed almost sane, and spoke in a most pathetic manner of her grave and the probability of the sun shining on it early in the morning, and her mother walking on it later in the day. At other times her malady would seize her, and she would snatch the brick off the string and throw it fiercely at Tennyson. Once, in an uncontrollable fit of madness, she gave her sister Effie a half-share in her garden tools and an interest in a box of mignonette.

The poet stayed doggedly on. In the chill of the morning twilight he broke the ice in his water-basin and cursed the girl. But he felt that he had broken the ice and he stayed.

On the whole, life at the cottage, though rugged, was not cheerless. In the long winter evenings they would gather around a smoking fire of peat, while Tennyson read aloud the *Idylls of the King* to the rude old cottager.

Not to show his rudeness, the old man kept awake by sitting on a tin-tack. This also kept his mind on the right tack. The two found that they had much in common, especially the old cottager. They called each other "Alfred" and "Hezekiah" now.

PART III

Time moved on and spring came.

Still the girl baffled the poet.

"I thought to pass away before," she would say with a mocking grin, "but yet alive I am, Alfred, alive I am."

Tennyson was fast losing hope.

Worn out with early rising, they engaged a retired Pullman-car porter to take up his quarters, and being a negro his presence added a touch of colour to their life.

The poet also engaged a neighbouring divine at fifty cents an evening to read to the child the best hundred books, with explanations. The May Queen tolerated him, and used to like to play with his silver hair, but protested that he was prosy.

At the end of his resources the poet resolved upon desperate measures.

He chose an evening when the cottager and his wife were out at a dinner-party.

At nightfall Tennyson and his accomplices entered the girl's room.

She defended herself savagely with her brick, but was overpowered.

The negro seated himself upon her chest, while the clergyman hastily read a few verses about the comfort of early rising at the last day.

As he concluded, the poet drove his pen into her eye.

"Last call!" cried the negro porter triumphantly.

III. OLD MR. LONGFELLOW ON BOARD THE *HESPERUS*

"It was the schooner *Hesperus* that sailed the wintry sea,
And the skipper had taken his little daughter to bear him company."

There were but three people in the cabin party of the *Hesperus*: old Mr. Longfellow, the skipper, and the skipper's daughter.

The skipper was much attached to the child, owing to the singular whiteness of her skin and the exceptionally limpid blue of her eyes; she had hitherto remained on shore to fill lucrative engagements as albino lady in a circus.

This time, however, her father had taken her with him for company. The girl was an endless source of amusement to the skipper and the crew. She constantly got up games of puss-in-the-corner, forfeits, and Dumb Crambo with her father and Mr. Longfellow, and made Scripture puzzles and geographical acrostics for the men.

Old Mr. Longfellow was taking the voyage to restore his shattered nerves. From the first the captain disliked Henry. He was utterly unused to the sea and was nervous and fidgety in the extreme. He complained that at sea his genius had not a sufficient degree of latitude. Which was unparalleled presumption.

On the evening of the storm there had been a little jar between Longfellow and the captain at dinner. The captain had emptied it several times, and was consequently in a reckless, quarrelsome humour.

"I confess I feel somewhat apprehensive," said old

Henry nervously, "of the state of the weather. I have had some conversation about it with an old gentleman on deck who professed to have sailed the Spanish main. He says you ought to put into yonder port."

"I have," hiccoughed the skipper, eyeing the bottle, and added with a brutal laugh that he "could weather the roughest gale that ever wind did blow." A whole Gaelic society, he said, wouldn't fizz on him.

Draining a final glass of grog, he rose from his chair, said grace, and staggered on deck.

All the time the wind blew colder and louder.

The billows frothed like yeast. It was a yeast wind.

The evening wore on.

Old Henry shuffled about the cabin in nervous misery.

The skipper's daughter sat quietly at the table selecting verses from a Biblical clock to amuse the ship's bosun, who was suffering from toothache.

At about ten Longfellow went to his bunk, requesting the girl to remain up in his cabin.

For half an hour all was quiet, save the roaring of the winter wind.

Then the girl heard the old gentleman start up in bed.

"What's that bell, what's that bell?" he gasped.

A minute later he emerged from his cabin wearing a cork jacket and trousers over his pyjamas.

"Sissy," he said, "go up and ask your pop who rang that bell."

The obedient child returned.

"Please, Mr. Longfellow," she said, "pa says there weren't no bell."

The old man sank into a chair and remained with his head buried in his hands.

"Say," he exclaimed presently, "someone's firing

guns and there's a glimmering light somewhere. You'd better go upstairs again."

Again the child returned.

"The crew are guessing at an acrostic, and occasionally they get a glimmering of it."

Meantime the fury of the storm increased.

The skipper had the hatches battered down.

Presently Longfellow put his head out of a porthole and called out, "Look here, you may not care, but the cruel rocks are goring the sides of this boat like the horns of an angry bull."

The brutal skipper heaved the log at him. A knot in it struck a plank and it glanced off.

Too frightened to remain below, the poet raised one of the hatches by picking out the cotton batting and made his way on deck. He crawled to the wheelhouse.

The skipper stood lashed to the helm all stiff and stark. He bowed stiffly to the poet. The lantern gleamed through the gleaming snow on his fixed and glassy eyes. The man was hopelessly intoxicated.

All the crew had disappeared. When the missile thrown by the captain had glanced off into the sea, they glanced after it and were lost.

At this moment the final crash came.

Something hit something. There was an awful click followed by a peculiar grating sound, and in less time than it takes to write it (unfortunately), the whole wreck was over.

As the vessel sank, Longfellow's senses left him. When he reopened his eyes he was in his own bed at home, and the editor of his local paper was bending over him.

"You have made a first-rate poem of it, Mr. Longfellow," he was saying, unbending somewhat as he spoke, "and I am very happy to give you our cheque for a dollar and a quarter for it."

"Your kindness checks my utterance," murmured Henry feebly, very feebly.

A, B, AND C

THE HUMAN ELEMENT IN MATHEMATICS

THE student of arithmetic who has mastered the first four rules of his art, and successfully striven with money sums and fractions, finds himself confronted by an unbroken expanse of questions known as problems. These are short stories of adventure and industry with the end omitted, and though betraying a strong family resemblance, are not without a certain element of romance.

The characters in the plot of a problem are three people called A, B, and C. The form of the question is generally of this sort:

"A, B, and C do a certain piece of work. A can do as much work in one hour as B in two, or C in four. Find how long they work at it."

Or thus:

"A, B, and C are employed to dig a ditch. A can dig as much in one hour as B can dig in two, and B can dig twice as fast as C. Find how long, etc., etc."

Or after this wise:

"A lays a wager that he can walk faster than B or C. A can walk half as fast again as B, and C is only an indifferent walker. Find how far, and so forth."

The occupations of A, B, and C are many and varied. In the older arithmetics they contented themselves with doing "a certain piece of work." This statement of the case, however, was found too sly and mysterious, or possibly lacking in romantic charm. It became the fashion to define the job more clearly and to set them at walking-matches, ditch-digging, regattas, and piling cord wood. At times they became commercial and entered into partnership, having with their old mystery a "certain" capital. Above all they revel in motion. When they tire of walking-matches—A rides on horseback, or borrows a bicycle and competes with his weaker-minded associates on foot. Now they race on locomotives; now they row; or again they become historical and engage stage-coaches; or at times they are aquatic and swim. If their occupation is actual work they prefer to pump water into cisterns, two of which leak through holes in the bottom and one of which is water-tight. A, of course, has the good one; he also takes the bicycle, and the best locomotive, and the right of swimming with the current. Whatever they do they put money on it, being all three sports. A always wins.

In the early chapters of the arithmetic, their identity is concealed under the names John, William, and Henry, and they wrangle over the division of marbles. In algebra they are often called X, Y, and Z. But these are only their Christian names, and they are really the same people.

Now to one who has followed the history of these men through countless pages of problems, watched them in their leisure hours dallying with cord wood, and seen their panting sides heave in the full frenzy of filling a cistern with a leak in it, they become something more than mere symbols. They appear as creatures of flesh and blood, living men with their own passions, ambitions, and aspirations like the rest of us. Let us view them in turn. A is a full-blooded blustering fellow, of energetic temperament, hot-headed and strong-willed. It is he who proposes everything, challenges B to work, makes the bets, and bends the others to his will. He is a man of great physical strength and phenomenal endurance. He has been known to walk forty-eight hours at a stretch, and to pump ninety-six. His life is arduous and full of peril. A mistake in the working of a sum may keep him digging a fortnight without sleep. A repeating decimal in the answer might kill him.

B is a quiet, easy-going fellow, afraid of A and bullied by him, but very gentle and brotherly to little C, the weakling. He is quite in A's power, having lost all his money in bets.

Poor C is an undersized, frail man, with a plaintive face. Constant walking, digging, and pumping has broken his health and ruined his nervous system. His joyless life has driven him to drink and smoke more than is good for him, and his hand often shakes as he digs ditches. He has not the strength to work as the others can, in fact, as Hamlin Smith has said, "A can do more work in one hour than C in four."

The first time that ever I saw these men was one evening after a regatta. They had all been rowing in it, and it had transpired that A could row as much in one hour as B in two, or C in four. B and C had come in dead fagged and C was coughing badly. "Never mind, old fellow," I heard B say, "I'll fix you up on the sofa and get you some hot tea." Just then A came blustering in and shouted, "I say, you fellows, Hamlin Smith has shown me three cisterns in his garden and he says we can pump them until tomorrow night. I bet I can beat you both. Come on. You can pump in your rowing things, you know. Your cistern leaks a little, I think, C." I heard

B growl that it was a dirty shame and that C was used up now, but they went, and presently I could tell from the sound of the water that A was pumping four times as fast as C.

For years after that I used to see them constantly about town and always busy. I never heard of any of them eating or sleeping. Then owing to a long absence from home, I lost sight of them. On my return I was surprised to no longer find A, B, and C at their accustomed tasks; on inquiry I heard that work in this line was now done by N, M, and O, and that some people were employing for algebraical jobs four foreigners called Alpha, Beta, Gamma, and Delta.

Now it chanced one day that I stumbled upon old D, in the little garden in front of his cottage, hoeing in the sun. D is an aged labouring man who used occasionally to be called in to help A, B, and C. "Did I know 'em, sir?" he answered. "Why, I knowed 'em ever since they was little fellows in brackets. Master A, he were a fine lad, sir, though I always said, give me Master B for kind-heartedness-like. Many's the job as we've been on together, sir, though I never did no racing nor aught of that, but just the plain labour, as you might say. I'm getting a bit too old and stiff for it nowadays, sir—just scratch about in the garden here and grow a bit of a logarithm, or raise a common denominator or two. But Mr. Euclid he use me still for them propositions, he do."

From the garrulous old man I learned the melancholy end of my former acquaintances. Soon after I left town, he told me, C had been taken ill. It seems that A and B had been rowing on the river for a wager, and C had been running on the bank and then sat in a draught. Of course the bank had refused the draught and C was taken ill. A and B came home and found C lying helpless in bed. A shook him roughly and said, "Get up, C, we're going to pile wood." C looked so worn and pitiful that B said, "Look here, A, I won't stand this, he isn't fit to pile wood to-night." C smiled feebly and said, "Perhaps I might pile a little if I sat up in bed." Then B, thoroughly alarmed, said, "See here, A, I'm going to fetch a doctor; he's dying." A flared up and answered, "You've no money to fetch a doctor." "I'll reduce him to his lowest terms," B said firmly, "that'll fetch him." C's life might even then have been saved but they made a mistake about the medicine. It stood at the head of the bed on a bracket, and the nurse accidentally removed it from the bracket without changing the sign. After the fatal blunder C seems to have sunk rapidly. On the evening of the next day, as the shadows deepened in the little room, it was clear to all that the end was near. I think that even A was affected at the last as he stood with bowed head, aimlessly offering to bet with the doctor on C's laboured breathing. "A," whispered C, "I think I'm going fast." "How fast do you think you'll go, old man?" murmured A. "I don't know," said C, "but I'm going at any rate."—The end came soon after that. C rallied for a moment and asked for a certain piece of work that he had left downstairs. A put it in his arms and he expired. As his soul sped heavenward A watched its flight with melancholy admiration. B burst into a passionate flood of tears and sobbed, "Put away his little cistern and the rowing clothes he used to wear. I feel as if I could hardly ever dig again."—The funeral was plain and unostentatious. It differed in nothing from the ordinary, except that out of deference to sporting men and mathematicians, A engaged two hearses. Both vehicles started at the same time, B driving the one which bore the sable parallelopiped containing the last remains of his ill-fated friend. A on the box of the empty hearse generously consented to a handicap of a hundred yards, but arrived first at the cemetery by driving four times as fast as B. (Find the distance to the cemetery.) As the sarcophagus was lowered, the grave was surrounded by the broken figures of the first book of Euclid.—It was noticed that after the death of C, A became a changed man. He lost interest in racing with B, and dug but languidly. He finally gave up his work and settled down to live on the interest of his bets.—B never recovered from the shock of C's death; his grief preyed upon his intellect and it became deranged. He grew moody and spoke only in monosyllables. His disease became rapidly aggravated, and he presently spoke only in words whose spelling was regular and which presented no difficulty to the beginner. Realising his precarious condition he voluntarily submitted to be incarcerated in an asylum, where he abjured mathematics and devoted himself to writing the History of the Swiss Family Robinson in words of one syllable.

Afterword

BY ROBERTSON DAVIES

Literary Lapses was Stephen Leacock's first book, and he published it himself in 1910, when he was forty. It may seem odd to us now that he should have begun his career as an author so late in life, but we must remember that in his twenties and thirties he was busily engaged in fitting himself for work as a university professor; this meant some years of teaching school, which he greatly disliked, and study at the University of Chicago for the Ph.D., which made him eligible for a university appointment. During his thirties he did a great deal of writing on history and political science, and also wrote occasional light articles and sketches for the periodical press. He does not seem to have thought of these as comprising the better part of his literary output, or as marking the channel in which the best of his talent would flow. But in 1910 he gathered his fugitive pieces together and had them printed by the Gazette Printing Company of Montreal; it appears to have been his notion that this book, offered for sale on railway news stands, might be welcome to travellers in search of light entertainment.

The book quickly found its way into the hands of John Lane, of the Bodley Head publishing house in London; Lane was at that time rising toward the crest of his wave as a publisher of strongly individual character and unusual taste; within the year he had brought out a much more professional edition of the book in England, and in 1911 this was followed by *Nonsense Novels*. Leacock was launched on his career as a popular, best-selling humorist.

The first edition of *Literary Lapses* is now rare. It is a pleasant little book, bound in green boards with a green buckram spine, to which the title is fixed on a buff label. It contains one hundred and twenty-five pages of good paper with a deckle edge; and adorning the first page, above "My Financial Career," is an engraving of a bookshelf of Edwardian sinuosity, containing seventeen books of that unreadable appearance which is supposed by artists to go with guaranteed literary worth; quite plainly none of these is a work of humour. In a modest preface the author acknowledges permission to republish given by *Truth* of New York, *Punch*, *Puck*, *Life*, *The Lancet*, and *Saturday Night* of Toronto. He also lets it be known that his sketches have been "frequently reprinted," which means that they had been widely stolen, for those were days when authors had little recourse against such piracy, and had to take it as a compliment. The price of the book was thirty-five cents – a sum which raised it above the vulgarity of ten and twenty-five-cent "railway" books, but did not thrust it into the elegant company of the fifty-centers.

In considering Leacock's work as a whole, it is interesting to observe that his humorous writing does not vary greatly in quality; though *Literary Lapses* is his first book it contains some of his best work. His books on serious subjects were of uneven merit, but his fountain of humour seems to have bubbled with strength and clarity all through his life. "My Financial Career," in which he writes of the embarrassment of a man opening a bank account, is as sure in touch as anything he wrote at any time in his life. "Boarding-House Geometry," written by a man who had lived in seventeen different Toronto boarding-houses during his student days, could not be improved by the addition or subtraction of a single word. So also with "A, B, and C"; children of today still find it extremely funny, though methods of teaching arithmetic have changed radically in fifty years. These pieces seize immediately upon the reader and move him to laughter, though they speak of a time which is now long past. The fact that Leacock's humour sets time at nought is one of the most telling proofs that it is humour of genius.

Most of what appears in this book is mined from his golden vein, but there are exceptions. "Number Fifty-Six" is all very well, and we can still read it with pleasure, but it is fun in the mode of an era which has gone; it shows us Leacock in one of his rare moods of imitation; stuff like "Number Fifty-Six" was to be found in all the funny magazines at the turn of the century and, like most humour which follows a formula, it has had its day.

There is nothing dated, however, about "Telling His Faults," or "The Awful Fate of Melpomenus Jones"; beautiful girls are not encountered as often at summer hotels as they were in Leacock's time, for the summer hotel as such has lost its hold on the public; but beautiful girls still use the technique which brought Mr. Sapling to their feet. And which of us, not born with a soul of brass, has not feared that he might suffer the fate of Melpomenus Jones? As for "The Conjurer's Revenge," is there anyone who has spoken, or acted, or played on a musical instrument, or in any way striven to entertain the public, who has not learned to spot the Quick Man in each audience, and to wish that he might revenge himself ruthlessly upon this enemy of humankind?

Leacock's humour avoided the tiresomeness of formulas and repetitions because it was truly an emanation of his own remarkable character. Though he owed something to Dickens and Mark Twain, he was no imitator. Not only was he very funny on paper; he was much funnier in his own person. The word which occurs again and again in newspaper accounts of his lecture tours is "fun." It is a word which is a little out of favour at present, for this is not an age in which simple fun is much understood or valued. In our day, humour has become, as never before, a marketable commodity, created and sold by committees of industrious, ulcerous, clever but basically humourless men, to the movies, the radio, and television. Much of what passes as humour today is this manufactured stuff, supported by the synthetic clangour of empty laughter from studio audiences. We have also a brittle, egghead wit, so fast and wry and nervous that it is exhausting rather than refreshing in its effect. But of fun – fun in the sense in which the Edwardians used the word – we have very little.

Leacock was a master of fun. He convulsed his audiences by a flow of nonsense which seemed so wonderfully easy that nobody sought to analyse how it was created. In *My Discovery of England* he tells how he almost killed a man in an English audience with laughing. This account is only slightly exaggerated. People who went to Leacock's lectures laughed until they hurt themselves; they laughed until mildly disgraceful personal misfortunes befell them. And Leacock laughed with them. He delighted in their laughter and he gloried in his own power to provoke it. There was nothing of the dry humorist or the pawky joker about him. He was plenteous and bountiful in his evocation of laughter. He was in the greatest tradition, not of wit, not of irony or sarcasm, but of true, deep humour, the full and joyous recognition of the Comic Spirit at work in life.

This is not the place to discuss the special cast of temperament which makes a man a humorist. It is enough to say that a man who is a great humorist, as Leacock was, is a man of unusual breadth of sympathy, and that the extension of feeling which gives him a strong sense of the comic at one end of his emotional range, is balanced by an understanding of what is tragic at the other end of the scale. Leacock wrote remarkable comic books, and he was a master of the exceedingly difficult art of comic lecturing. But it would not have needed a very great shift in the foundations of his temperament to have made him a writer of tragedies.

For this reason we do ill if we consider him, in our Canadian literature, as a funny-man, to be esteemed below other writers who have chosen tragic or pastoral happenings upon which to rest their work. He was a great writer – one of the greatest we have ever possessed.

In *Literary Lapses* you hold the first work of a man who was to achieve great fame as a writer. But there is about it nothing of the 'prentice hand; Leacock's apprenticeship to the hard craft of humour was contemporaneous with those hateful days of schoolmastering and living the life of a poor student at the University of Toronto. *Literary Lapses* is, in the true sense of the word, a masterpiece – which is to say, the work which the apprentice offers at the end of his training and which shows him to be a master indeed.

BY STEPHEN LEACOCK

AUTOBIOGRAPHY

The Boy I Left Behind Me (1946)

BIOGRAPHY

Mark Twain (1932)

Charles Dickens: His Life and Work (1933)

DRAMA

"Q": A Farce in One Act [with Basil Macdonald] (1915)

ECONOMICS

Economic Prosperity in the British Empire (1930)

Back to Prosperity:
The Great Opportunity of the Empire Conference (1932)

The Gathering Financial Crisis in Canada:
A Survey of the Present Critical Situation (1936)

EDUCATION

The Pursuit of Knowledge: A Discussion of Freedom and Compulsion in Education (1934)

Too Much College, or Education Eating Up Life (1939)

HISTORY

Baldwin, Lafontaine, Hincks:
Responsible Government (1907)

Adventures of the Far North:
A Chronicle of the Frozen Seas (1914)
The Dawn of Canadian History: A Chronicle of Aboriginal Canada and the Coming of the White Man (1914)
The Mariner of St. Malo:
A Chronicle of the Voyages of Jacques Cartier (1914)
Mackenzie, Baldwin, Lafontaine, Hincks (1926)
Lincoln Frees the Slaves (1934)
The British Empire:
Its Structure, Its History, Its Strength (1940)
Canada: The Foundations of Its Future (1941)
Our Heritage of Liberty: Its Origin, Its Achievement, Its Crisis: A Book for War Time (1942)
Montreal: Seaport and City (1942)
Canada and the Sea (1944)

HUMOUR

Literary Lapses (1910)
Nonsense Novels (1911)
Sunshine Sketches of a Little Town (1912)
Behind the Beyond, and Other Contributions to Human Knowledge (1913)
Arcadian Adventures with the Idle Rich (1914)
Moonbeams from the Larger Lunacy (1915)
Further Foolishness:
Sketches and Satires on the Follies of the Day (1916)
Frenzied Fiction (1918)
The Hohenzollerns in America: with the Bolsheviks in Berlin, and Other Impossibilities (1919)
Winsome Winnie, and Other New Nonsense Novels (1920)
My Discovery of England (1922)
College Days (1923)
Over the Footlights (1923)
The Garden of Folly (1924)
Winnowed Wisdom: A New Book of Humour (1926)
Short Circuits (1928)

The Iron Man and the Tin Woman, with Other Such Futurities (1929)
Wet Wit and Dry Humour: Distilled from the Pages of Stephen Leacock (1931)
The Dry Pickwick and Other Incongruities (1932)
Afternoons in Utopia: Tales of the New Time (1932)
Hellements of Hickonomics in Hiccoughs of Verse Done in Our Social Planning Mill (1936)
Funny Pieces: A Book of Random Sketches (1936)
Here Are My Lectures (1937)
Model Memoirs, and Other Sketches from Simple to Serious (1938)
My Remarkable Uncle, and Other Sketches (1942)
Happy Stories, Just to Laugh At (1943)
Last Leaves (1945)

LITERARY CRITICISM

Essays and Literary Studies (1916)
Humour: Its Theory and Technique (1935)
The Greatest Pages of American Humor (1936)
Humour and Humanity: An Introduction to the Study of Humour (1937)
How to Write (1943)

POLITICAL SCIENCE

Elements of Political Science (1906)
The Unsolved Riddle of Social Justice (1920)
My Discovery of the West: A Discussion of East and West in Canada (1937)
While There Is Time: The Case against Social Catastrophe (1945)